# camp pain

Travel Writer Mystery Series - 1

**wendy meadows**

Majestic Owl Publishing LLC
P.O. Box 997
Newport, NH 03773

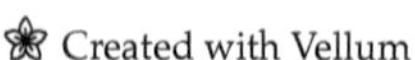

Created with Vellum

# chapter one

Patricia rolled down the window of her RV as she drove south into Georgia and breathed in the warm spring air. Patricia had left cold, snowy New York City yesterday morning and after one night at a campground in Roanoke, Virginia the night before, she was happy to see the green landscape around her, crawling with kudzu and bursting into flower.

She sang along with the radio, her curly red hair waving in the wind, enjoying the freedom of life in her RV. There was nothing better than this, Patricia knew—the excitement of hitting the open road whenever she wanted, off on an adventure where she would explore a new place. Patricia was a woman with a gypsy soul who loved meeting new people and meeting new adventures head-on, which was why her career as a travel writer was so satisfying to her.

Patricia was coming to the end of a fourteen-hour drive. Her editor and publisher had planned out her travel writing assignments and wanted her to write a long feature article about Atlanta. Before New York, Patricia had been in Philadelphia researching a similar feature, and, despite the cold, she had had a blast doing it. She took a deep breath of the warm, fresh air blowing in through her window now and could hardly wait to see what Atlanta had to offer her.

Patricia kept her attention on the highway, humming along softly to the classic rock song playing on her radio. A small sporty car zoomed past her on the right. Patricia smiled. *I'll probably see them pulled over in a few minutes,* she thought. Sure enough, a few miles down the road Patricia saw the sleek red car next to a sheriff's car with its lights flashing. Patricia's RV could manage a good speed, but she generally kept to the posted limits. As a young woman, she had worked a clerical job at a police station processing tickets and citations, and she had a healthy respect for the law. She had no desire to add a speeding ticket to her life achievements.

Of course, once she had been promoted to administrative assistant to the detectives there, she had wished to add plenty of things to her life achievements. Her writing skills and people skills were unparalleled—she had her degree in English and Psychology to thank for that—but she lacked the credentials to do more than help out occasionally with investigations. "You have talent, kid," a detective sergeant had once told her. "Call me when you've got a badge to back it up. Until then, stick to your paperwork." It stung. But truthfully, Patricia knew she would be a little miserable if she went to the police academy. Her free spirit longed for something more. That very same week she had begun hunting for travel writing jobs, then sold her car to buy the RV not long after that.

Patricia knew she had made the right choice in life because when she saw the "Welcome to Georgia" sign, her heart sang. Patricia was almost at her destination. She would be staying at a campground next to a tourist attraction called Stone Mountain. There was plenty to explore there, plus a bus line ran from the park to Atlanta and nearby suburbs. That was perfect for Patricia, who relied on busses, taxis, and Ubers to get around.

A couple of hours later, Patricia was awed to see Stone Mountain rising tall in the middle of flat land and highways. It was beautiful. Patricia pulled up to the ranger station by the entrance. The ranger gave her a map showing her camping spot and welcomed her to the park. Patricia thanked him, and he wished her a good day in a sweet Georgia accent that made her grin.

Driving through the campground, the lush green trees rose on every side and families and couples walked along the paths. She found her space, parked and got out. Patricia hooked up her RV to the electric station and decided to stretch her legs after her long drive. The generator could charge while she took a walk. After donning her favorite floppy straw hat to keep the sun out of her eyes, Patricia hopped out of her RV and locked the door. Even though campgrounds were generally safe, Patricia knew she was better safe than sorry. She may have a gypsy soul, but she also prided herself on being a savvy, careful traveler.

Patricia consulted the map of the park and set out toward a good walking trail. She walked along the small paved road and saw a young couple setting up their RV in a space nearby. The young man looked up and waved at Patricia. Patricia waved back.

"Hello," said the young man. He was dressed in shorts and a polo shirt. He had wavy brown hair and a friendly look.

"Hello, neighbor," responded Patricia. She stopped to chat, and he walked over. "I'm in the next lot over. My name is Patricia."

"My name is Tom," he said as they shook hands. She saw chairs and a table set up by the firepit. A pretty young woman walked up, her brown hair framing her face in fetching natural curls. "This is my wife, Valerie."

"It is nice to meet you both," said Patricia, and Valerie shook her hand warmly.

"Did you just arrive?" Valerie said.

"Yes. I just drove down from Virginia. Are you enjoying Stone Mountain so far?" Patricia asked.

"Yes," said Valerie with a huge grin. "We love it. We're on our honeymoon," she said and blushed a little, reaching out to hold Tom's hand.

"Yes, we are traveling all around the United States," Tom explained. "The RV was a wedding present from my uncle."

"How wonderful," exclaimed Patricia. "Congratulations on your wedding."

"How about you? What brings you here to Georgia?" asked Valerie.

"I am a travel writer, so my work brings me to Atlanta. My friends always tease me how much I love the RV life. My job is perfect for me. I guess I'm just a gypsy at heart." The young couple laughed.

"This seems like a really nice place to start your research. Quite a lot of things to do around the park, even before you head into Atlanta," said Tom.

"I thought so too," said Patricia. "Well, it was nice meeting you both. I am just stretching my legs on the trails. I'll let you get back to setting up."

"Okay," said Valerie. She hesitated, then added, "Later on we are headed to the famous Dekalb Farmer's Market. Would you like to join us? If it won't keep you from your work, that is."

"Thank you," said Patricia, touched by the friendly gesture. "I would love to join you. The Dekalb market is actually on my list of must-see places." She could tell Valerie and Tom were the kind of campground neighbors she would enjoy making friends with.

"Great! Does four pm work?" Valerie asked.

"That works for me," said Patricia. "See you then." With a wave, she headed off toward the walking trail.

Patricia had read about Stone Mountain online and knew

it would be a great hook for her article about Atlanta. Anyone could write about Atlanta, but Patricia loved the unexpected angle of starting out a city visit from a secluded, lush park in the country. She was excited to see the famous carvings on the mountain, but the trail was so beautiful she almost forgot what was waiting for her at the top. The cherry tree blossoms wafted a delicate scent on the afternoon air, and purple blooms of wisteria draped on a grove of pecan trees along a creek by the trail.

Patricia climbed up the steep, smooth mountain trail. About thirty minutes later, she reached the top and caught her breath. Her hike was worth it. Patricia gasped at the sweeping view of the Atlanta skyline. She saw the Appalachian Trail and the lake below the mountain and stunning views in every direction.

Realizing it was nearly time to head back, Patricia noticed a cable car platform by the gift shop. She walked over and was told she could use her park pass for free rides up and down. *I wish I had known that before I hiked up here,* thought Patricia ruefully, but then realized she was grateful for the exercise. This way she could also describe the experience better in her article. Patricia rode down in the cable car, which provided a view of the carved monument.

When she reached the bottom, Patricia sauntered along the trail toward her RV and observed the wildlife. A small lizard scurried across the trail and it was followed by a slightly larger black snake. Patricia gasped a little, but she had done her homework on the wildlife of Georgia and she knew the black snake was non-venomous. Besides, snakes ate campground pests like mice and rats.

Back at her RV, Patricia hopped into the shower. While she scrubbed off the remains of travel and hiking, she reflected on a cute family she had seen at the top of Stone Mountain. Two boys wearing *I Survived the Stone Mountain Climb* t-shirts had made goofy faces while their parents took their pictures in front of the cable car sign. One boy took out a cell phone and took a selfie in front of the view and his brother held up two fingers to give him rabbit ears at the last second. Patricia laughed, remembering it.

She headed over to Tom and Valerie's campsite still thinking about that family, and she realized she knew exactly how she would start the write-up about Stone Mountain: *When's the last time your family took a selfie on a cable car 825 feet in the air?* She grinned.

When Tom pulled the car up to the Dekalb Farmer's Market, Patricia was surprised to see it was a rather unexciting brown warehouse, but when they stepped inside the doors, she gasped with surprise. Flags from every country in the world hung from the ceiling and aisle after aisle was lined with colorful bins of local produce and flowers from all over the country, as well as imported foods and delicacies.

What a sight. They even had a small buffet-style restaurant in the market that featured food from the marketplace. Patricia was overwhelmed by the variety of food available, but she gripped her shopping cart and got to work, waving merrily to Tom and Valerie who set off in the other direction. She started down the dry goods aisle and picked up some hibiscus tea, then in the produce section, she found prickly pear cactus next to the baby bok choy. Patricia's mouth watered, remembering an omelet with stir-fried cactus she had eaten in Las Vegas. She added it to her cart, determined to recreate that dish.

By the time she found Tom and Valerie again, her cart held bagels that rivaled the ones she had eaten in New York City, homemade quiches, organic milk in a glass bottle, and farmer's cheese.

"This place is amazing," Valerie gushed, coming over to admire Patricia's finds.

Tom was waiting for some lamb kebabs to be cut up and packaged at the meat counter.

"Tom always buys enough to feed an army," said Valerie with a laugh. "Patricia, you should join us tonight! I insist."

"You're too kind. How about I bring the dessert?" said Patricia. Tom and Valerie thought that sounded delicious and agreed.

Valerie and Patricia walked side by side with their carts, chatting amiably about dinner plans, when suddenly someone knocked into Patricia hard, jostling her shoulder. Patricia exclaimed and stumbled into Valerie. She rubbed her shoulder and looked up to see a man glowering at her as if it was her fault.

The man was tall with a shock of wavy brown hair that fell over his forehead. His serious blue eyes frowned down at her. "You should be more careful," he said in a warning tone.

*How rude,* Patricia thought. "Excuse me," she replied, mustering all the politeness she could manage. "You stumbled into me." She boldly stared him down.

He seemed surprised by her reply. But then he walked away, his eyes darting around in the crowd. As an afterthought, he said over his shoulder to her, "You should watch your purse, miss. There are pickpockets here sometimes." She watched his tall figure disappear swiftly into the market.

"What was that about?" Valerie said in bafflement. Her husband had picked up on the stranger's meaning, however.

"Check your purse," Tom said to Patricia with concern. Patricia was surprised to find her purse zipper open. Her pulse jumped in fear. She knew that pickpockets often tried to distract their targets while taking something.

"Well, if he's a thief, he's a really bad one. Nothing is missing," Patricia said with a sigh of relief.

"He didn't even apologize for knocking you over," said Valerie.

Patricia thought for a moment. Perhaps they were jumping to conclusions. He had simply warned her, after all. "Maybe we shouldn't judge a book by its cover," she said.

They headed for the check-out lanes. Patricia thought to herself that she would rather have a rude stranger than a thieving pickpocket, any day. Still, it left a sour feeling in her stomach, and she was happy when they were back in the car returning to the beautiful campground.

# chapter two

When they pulled up to Patricia's RV site at the Stone Mountain campground, Tom helped Patricia carry her bags of food to her RV, and she thanked the couple again for the ride to the market.

There were still a couple hours before dinner, and she needed to bake the dessert and take notes for her article. She waved as Tom and Valerie's car moved slowly down the campground road to the parking spot next to their RV.

Patricia put away her groceries, savoring the unexpected finds from the Dekalb Farmer's Market. She took out her cutting board and began to chop strawberries and rhubarb while her small but efficient oven heated up. When she popped the fruit cobbler in the oven to bake, it filled her home with a sweet smell. Patricia wrote down her notes about her adventures in Georgia so far, then changed into some warmer clothes before dinner.

Tom stood in front of the barbecue turning the savory kebabs on the coals. It smelled heavenly. Patricia and Valerie sat in comfortable camp chairs near the fire trading stories about their journeys so far. "One thing I have enjoyed about our honeymoon is getting to meet new people," said Valerie. "Most people are sweet and kind like you, though occasionally you do meet some strange ones." She shook her head, and Patricia knew she was thinking about the rude stranger in the market.

"I understand," said Patricia. "There was this one man I met on my travels who stalked me for a couple of days. I had to call the police. It was horrible."

"Did the police do anything?" Valerie asked.

"Yes. Fortunately, he had a previous record, so they arrested him," said Patricia, shivering. "It is times like that when I question my career choice. Fortunately, those times are few and far between."

"That is why I'm glad Tom and I are traveling together," said Valerie, smiling up at her handsome husband. "You are very brave traveling around by yourself. Where are you going after Atlanta?"

"My publisher has not told me yet," said Patricia. "When I find out, I will let you know."

"It would be fun if we could travel down to Key West together," said Valerie. Patricia agreed with her. She had never been to Key West, and it was one of the places she had always wanted to visit. *Maybe I can suggest that to my publisher,* Patricia thought.

Valerie set out a large bowl of salad filled with crisp veggies from the farmer's market. Tom brought the sizzling hot lamb kebabs to the picnic table, and they all sat down to enjoy the mouthwatering meal.

The young couple told Patricia that they had started their trip in Boston and were working their way south to Key West. After that, they were going to New Orleans and then across to California.

"We plan on getting our money's worth out of this honeymoon," Tom laughed.

"RV travel really is the best way to enjoy the country," said Valerie.

"It is one of the best perks of my job," Patricia agreed. They finished dinner and the young couple exclaimed happily when Patricia brought out the freshly-baked strawberry rhubarb dessert. They enjoyed the delicious fruit treat and then walked down the park road to watch the laser light show that danced across the face of Stone Mountain. Every night, the park created this spectacle for the visitors, and it truly made a beautiful contrast against the dark night sky. It was a beautiful end to such a wonderful dinner with her new friends.

Later that night, Patricia returned to her campsite and looked up at the stars. She felt lucky to be able to sit and watch them from her home. There were a few frogs croaking from a pond somewhere, crickets singing in the darkness, and an owl hooting in the far distance. The park felt cozy and safe at night, despite the velvety darkness. It seemed a lot darker now that the laser light show was done. Patricia shivered.

She had so much waiting for her in Atlanta the next day. She needed a good night's sleep. Patricia turned off all of the lights in the RV and found her bed by moonlight. The moon was almost full and shone through the little window by her bed. She lay down, and the chirping crickets lulled her to sleep.

In the morning, Patricia cooked an omelet for breakfast. She danced around the kitchen to the radio and planned out her day with excitement. There were still a few sights she wanted to check out at Stone Mountain before heading into Atlanta.

It was still early and cool when she walked over to the mountain. This time she rode the train around the base of the mountain. Patricia enjoyed the views and hopped out at the historic village and walked around looking at the historical houses. Actors in period clothing offered demonstrations of blacksmithing and churning butter. There was also a farmyard that taught children about raising livestock in the 1800s. Patricia stopped to pet a friendly goat and a donkey that nuzzled into her palm over the wooden fence.

After that, she headed for the city bus stop at the park entrance that would take her to her first stop, Decatur. A suburb of Georgia, Decatur was a hotspot of cultural and historical locations.

After her bus ride, she arrived in downtown Decatur. It boasted a fascinating variety of stores, including bookstores and a music shop. Patricia knew this was exactly the type of place her editor loved to see—a niche stop with unique finds, perfect for the antique lover and the quirky explorer.

Patricia looked in a small boutique and tried on some skirts. There was a silky scarf in the window that she thought would go perfectly with her favorite dress. The store attendant put her purchases in a bag so pretty it almost looked gift-wrapped.

On the sidewalk, many people strolled along enjoying the shopping and the sights. She loved to see people out walking their dogs, especially. Decatur seemed to be a haven for dog-lovers, as almost every store on the main street set out a bowl of water for their customers' pets.

Patricia visited the Carlos Museum at Emory University to see the artifacts and sculptures from Ancient Egypt. The museum also had exhibits from India and from Ancient Greece and Rome. The museum did not charge admission, and Patricia was impressed with the quality of their exhibits. It was like stepping into the past.

After the museum visit, Patricia wandered down the road to a bookstore and then to a music store. There she found a few good used CDs to add to her collection. She had an MP3 player and satellite radio in her RV, but she still liked the old-fashioned feel of putting in a CD and listening to an album start to finish. Since Patricia had started driving all over the country, she had learned the importance of good road music.

When the cashier rang up her selections, they had a quick discussion about local music and she came away with a few recommendations of places to see live local music. The friendly locals in Atlanta made this kind of small shop a perfect place for a weary traveler—always a smile for visitors. Not to mention she loved hearing those Georgia accents.

Patricia found a cute and casual restaurant in a stately two-story brick building on the main square and enjoyed a chicken pesto panini for lunch while she looked through a local arts newspaper. There were several upcoming shows that sounded good, and she wondered if Tom and Valerie might like to join her at a show later in the week.

As she strolled down the street with a salted caramel ice cream cone from the ice cream shop, Patricia hoped she could at least tempt her new friends with Decatur's culinary offerings. It was a true gem of a place. She headed for the MARTA bus stop and hopped on the next bus to Atlanta. Her next destination was the hip neighborhood of Little Five Points.

The bus let her off on a colorful, eclectic street that made her gypsy soul sing. Hand-painted sidewalk signs advertised little shops and pots of blooming flowers nestled among the tables at outdoor cafés. After window shopping and people-watching for a while, one of the neighborhood's landmarks caught her eye—the Vortex Bar, known for the giant skull at its entrance and its eye-popping décor. Needing a cool drink, Patricia headed there immediately and grinned to herself as she stepped through the jaw of the skull into the bar.

*This is the kind of place I love to write about,* thought Patricia as she entered the restaurant. Funky music played over the speakers, and the atmosphere was casual and fun. Patricia went to the bar and sat down. She ordered a drink and looked around. There were road signs, surfboards, license plates, vintage posters, and half of a motorcycle decorating the walls. There was even a shark head above the bar.

"Is this your first time here?" asked the bartender when he brought her drink.

"Is it that obvious?" laughed Patricia.

"Not too much," the bartender grinned back. He was about Patricia's age and had a couple of visible tattoos. He seemed friendly.

"Do you keep busy?" asked Patricia.

"Yes, we do," replied the bartender. "This place is hopping at night. We are known throughout the state for our burgers, too."

"Oh really?" asked Patricia.

"Yes. We've been featured on a couple of television shows for our burgers," replied the bartender as he pointed to some framed pictures behind the bar with a few television personalities Patricia recognized.

"What makes these burgers so special?" Patricia asked.

The bartender pointed to the burger page of the menu. Patricia read the menu and understood. The restaurant featured not just regular burgers, but mega-sized burgers as well. This place had a burger that was all different kinds of fun. It included a grilled cheese sandwich, bacon, and a fried egg.

"Has anyone ever finished one of these?" Patricia asked the bartender.

"A few people have, but not as many as order it," he said. Patricia laughed and ordered a small blue cheese burger. When it came, it was cooked just right. Patricia thanked the bartender for the chat. When she was done, she took a copy of the take-out menu with her so she could get down all the fascinating details when she wrote her article. She knew this place would be a hit with her editor.

That afternoon, Patricia put a lot of miles on her trusty

sneakers. She visited a number of downtown Atlanta spots like the aquarium, the CNN center, and the Olympics center. In her travels, she had perfected the art of visiting attractions and taking notes about their special features while she walked around. She would always snag a brochure or two with prices and hours for easy reference later.

As she exited the aquarium and packed another brochure into her small backpack, her phone buzzed with a message. It was from her editor, Lenore. *Patricia, I might have a huge assignment coming up for you,* Lenore wrote, *but I have to confirm a few details. I'll be in touch in a couple days! Enjoy Atlanta.* Patricia was intrigued. Lenore was not usually so mysterious. Patricia had put in a number of requests for future assignments, among them a hot air balloon festival in New Mexico, a Jazz festival in Key West, and even a stop in Washington D.C. complete with a White House tour. She crossed her fingers for good luck and sent back a message. *Thanks, Lenore! I can't wait to hear more.*

After such a packed day of sight-seeing and research for her article, Patricia was feeling tired, but her editor's mysterious message had given her a new burst of energy. She decided to head to one last stop before heading back to the campground—the Atlanta Botanical Garden.

The gardens teemed with visitors. The warm spring afternoon sun showed off the flowers and trees budding with color everywhere. Patricia stopped to admire a beautiful fountain and heard guitar music playing softly somewhere nearby. She climbed the stairs by the fountain, following the sound, and saw a family sitting on a picnic blanket. The father played a guitar. She thought she recognized it as an old Bob Dylan tune.

She was not the only one listening. A number of strolling visitors lingered to listen as the man played. Patricia thought it was the perfect moment to end the perfect day. When the song ended, the small crowd clapped appreciatively.

As she passed through the small crowd on her way toward the main gate, she saw a tall, brown-haired man looking at her strangely. She realized with a shock that it was the same handsome man she had seen at the farmer's market. *That's a strange coincidence,* she thought to herself. She looked back from a distance after she kept walking but did not see him again. She doubted she was being followed and reminded herself there was no evidence that he was a pickpocket. However, she held her purse close to her as she headed for the MARTA bus stop. Just in case.

Back at the campground, Tom and Valerie invited her over to share some beers around the campfire after dinner. She joined them and told them about the live music venues she discovered. "That sounds like fun," said Valerie.

"We were hoping to catch some good music in Atlanta," Tom added.

"There is a restaurant and bar at one of the live venues, and they seem to have some good acts coming up," said Patricia.

"Maybe we could all go and see a show," suggested Valerie.

"That sounds like a great idea," said Tom.

"I was hoping you'd want to go together," Patricia laughed. She did not want to impose on her new friends, but they were as eager for shared adventures as she was. They lingered around the fire telling stories. When Patricia yawned and said goodnight, Tom promised to tell her all about his uncle's blues band when they all went to the live show together.

"No blues band stories unless she tells us where to find that salted caramel ice cream," Valerie teased. Everyone laughed, and Patricia promised to show them all her favorite places when they went together. She waved to Tom and Valerie and walked down the dark, narrow road toward her RV.

Sleepy, she climbed into bed with a warm feeling of satisfaction. It had been an almost perfect day.

# chapter three

For her second full day in Atlanta, Patricia got up bright and early. Over coffee and breakfast, she listened to birdsong outside and checked the weather. She took out a light sweater to take with her for the day in case it became cold. On her way to the bus stop, she walked past Tom and Valerie's campsite and saw Valerie hanging a pretty windchime from the corner of their RV.

"That's so pretty, Val."

"Thanks! I'm collecting one from every stop on our honeymoon. By the time we settle down, our house will be the most musical on the block when the wind blows," said Valerie.

Patricia smiled, thinking of their future neighbors. "I was wondering if you wanted to meet tonight for dinner and a show?" said Patricia. "I checked the listings and a local musician named Ben is playing tonight and it seems like it would be a good show. I've seen some reviews of his albums online and I think his show will be really great."

"That sounds like a great idea," said Tom. Valerie agreed.

"Well, I am going to take the bus into town, so I will meet you both there around six. I'll text you the address. Will that work for you?" Patricia asked Tom.

"Yes, that will be perfect," said Tom.

"Okay. I will see you later," said Patricia, and she walked along the sunny road toward the bus stop. A breeze fluttered through the trees and chilled her a little. She was glad she had remembered to bring a sweater. She walked over to the bus station and only had to wait a few minutes for her bus downtown. Patricia had decided to visit the zoo.

When she arrived, Patricia noticed there were quite a few families there. She asked the ticket person about the number of younger children.

"This is family day at the zoo. Any children under 10 are admitted free today," said the woman in the booth.

"That is a nice idea," said Patricia, making a mental note to include that in her article. She imagined a family with young children would want to know about the zoo. She would also mention the children's play garden she had passed at the Botanical Garden the day before. The Botanical Garden reminded Patricia of the stranger she had seen twice so far, and she hoped he did not turn up again. She had half a mind to report him on suspicion of pickpocketing if she saw him for a third time. He always seemed to be around when there was a crowd, after all.

Patricia enjoyed exploring the zoo. She strolled through the grounds and spent some time at the panda enclosure. Patricia found out that many surrounding counties had volunteered to grow extra bamboo to help keep the pandas fed. Patricia also saw the Sumatran tiger exhibit. As she watched, the large striped feline stalked silently behind a tree and melted into the shadows. She shivered with delight and admiration. Patricia also enjoyed the monkey habitat and the reptile show. After that, Patricia decided it was time to go to her next destination. She got on a bus and went to the Fernbank Museum of Natural History.

This was a museum that catered to a younger crowd, but it interested Patricia. The huge dinosaur fossils were a big attraction. When she arrived, she decided to go explore the forest area. Two miles of trails led through the grounds with hands-on exhibits for children. Patricia watched a couple of children race up the trail to a pod-shaped lookout. Patricia enjoyed being around children. Their enthusiasm reminded her of the delights of travel. Patricia wandered back through the forest and into the museum to explore its large shell exhibit. She had a good time at the museum and did not realize how long she had been there until her stomach started to growl. She snacked on a protein bar from her backpack while she waited for the bus, planning out her next stop. Patricia had brought her tablet laptop with her so she could work on her article that afternoon and planned to visit a famous arts center with the charming name of the Goat Farm Art Collective. A few movies and television shows had used the repurposed mill building where it was located as a backdrop, and it hosted theatre and music events all year long.

When Patricia got there, she was tickled to find actual goats in the middle of Atlanta. She found a coffee shop and ordered a sandwich and a latté and settled in with her laptop. After about an hour, Patricia had typed up her notes and outlined the sections of her article. It was coming together nicely, even though she still had a lot to do. Atlanta was such a rich site for tourism, she knew her article would just scratch the surface, but it would be her own unique take on the city.

Finished with her work, she strolled around the location. What amazed her about the repurposed mill was that it was a green oasis in the middle of a bustling city. Patricia wandered around and saw some blacksmiths and dancers. She found out that some people lived there and others rented spaces. Atlanta was proving to be a truly eclectic city.

When she checked her watch, Patricia realized she had time for one more stop before meeting Tom and Valerie. She hopped a bus westward and visited the Jimmy Carter

Presidential Library. It was an amazing place to learn about civil rights history. By the time she had gone through the library, it was time for Patricia to get on a bus to meet Tom and Valerie.

When Patricia arrived at the venue, her friends were already there. Patricia saw them in the outdoor bar area. Valerie waved to her, and Patricia waved back. She stopped and bought a ticket to the performance and then joined the happy couple at their table.

"So, where did you wander today?" asked Valerie as she sipped her sweet tea.

"I went all around central Atlanta," said Patricia. She told them about the zoo and the farm. Tom and Valerie listened and told Patricia about their own visit to an art museum.

"I get tired thinking of all the places you have been," said Valerie. "I think my feet would be killing me if I walked that much."

"Well, I always wear sneakers when I wander," said Patricia. "You would be amazed how many pairs of sneakers I go through in a year. Now Tom, you promised me some good stories about your uncle's blues band." Tom kept them laughing through dinner with anecdotes about his Uncle Jake's traveling blues band in the seventies. By the time they finished their meal, the live music was starting up, so they all walked over to the stage area.

"He is quite good," said Valerie after the singer Ben's first song, which was modern rock and blues mixed with soulful acoustic songs.

"I love seeing up-and-coming artists in small venues like this," said Tom.

"Me too. Performances are so much more intimate than in a big arena," said Patricia. They all swayed a little to the music and enjoyed the performance through to the very end. They clapped loudly for the musician, who bowed and sang one encore song. After the show, Tom and Valerie offered Patricia a ride back to the campground.

"I will take you up on that," said Patricia. "Thank you."

Still excited by the show, they chatted all the way back to Stone Mountain. Patricia thanked them again for the ride and walked back to her RV. She was exhausted but happy. The stars twinkled in a few places, but clouds covered the moon so that the park was mostly dark shadows. She was surprised to see how late it was. When she got to her campsite, she plopped down in her outside chair. She heard a noise and turned her head. It was a little raccoon rummaging in the bushes. She had seen its footprints around her campsite. However, all she saw was its bushy tail as the raccoon rushed through the undergrowth by her RV.

"What are you running from?" Patricia asked the departing animal, stifling a yawn. Just then, she heard another noise. It sounded like it was coming from the road. It sounded like someone running, fast. That was strange because it was after 2 am, and most of the campground was fast asleep. She figured that someone had been startled by the raccoon. Her sleepiness fading, Patricia grabbed a flashlight.

"Tom? Valerie? Is that you?" Patricia called out quietly while walking toward the road.

Patricia walked in the direction of the footsteps. Patricia tried to step carefully. It occurred to her at the last moment that maybe a large animal lurked out there and had scared off both the running person and the raccoon. Perhaps she should have stayed in her RV until morning.

An owl hooted, and she turned to look, startled. Just then, her foot hit something, and Patricia tripped. She sprawled on the dewy grass. Patricia got herself up and found her flashlight. When she turned the light to find what had caused her to stumble, Patricia could not help but scream.

A few seconds later, Tom and Valerie appeared. They were in their pajamas and had their flashlights with them. Patricia yelled out to Valerie to stop where she was and call the police. She quickly shone her flashlight on the body so Tom could see what was happening. He then moved quickly to help Patricia get up and helped her back to her RV.

"What is going on?" asked Valerie. She followed them with the phone pressed to her ear.

"Do you have 911 on the line?" Tom insisted.

"Yes," said Valerie. Patricia motioned for the phone, and Valerie handed it to her. Valerie tuned pale and sat down on Patricia's RV steps as Patricia described what she had literally stumbled on.

"Yes, I found a body. I am pretty sure he is dead…I tripped over him and he did not move…Yes, I said tripped. Okay, thank you." Patricia hung up the phone and said the police would be there soon. Tom and Valerie offered to stay with her, and Patricia nodded, a little numb.

"Tom, could you look in my refrigerator? I have a pitcher of herbal iced tea in there. I bet we could all use a glass," said Patricia. She was still in shock, but she wanted to hold it together for Valerie's sake. Valerie was shivering, hunched on the picnic table bench. Tom got the tea and poured everyone a glass. He sat down next to Valerie and put his arm around her. They all sat in silence and waited for the police. After a minute, Patricia became antsy and decided to take a look at the body. She figured the more she could tell the police, the better.

Patricia carefully went back to where she found the body. It was a man, lying on his back. There was blood pooled by his chest and head. Patricia looked around a little more. The tall grass by the victim's feet was flattened out and bent. Patricia realized that the body had probably been dragged here from the road.

Moments later, one lone police car inched down the road. No lights, no siren. Patricia guessed they probably did not want to alarm the other campers and attract a crowd. A couple park rangers driving a golf cart followed the police car and stayed on the road to block any approaching traffic.

Tom went to the road and waved his flashlight to signal them. The police car parked by Tom's RV and Tom crossed over to talk to him. Patricia sat beside Valerie, waiting for the officer to arrive. Suddenly, the area was lit up. The officer had turned on his car lights and a searchlight mounted on his vehicle. Patricia held her hand up to her eyes until she adjusted to the brightness. When she put her hand down, there was an officer standing beside her. He was taller than Patricia and about her age, maybe a little bit older. He had dark, wavy brown hair and piercing blue eyes. The officer held out his hand to Patricia.

"Hello. I am Officer Brian Johnson. I'm a detective with the force. Are you Patricia?" the officer asked.

"Yes, I am," Patricia replied, shaking the officer's hand slowly. Confused for a moment, it suddenly dawned on her. She almost did not recognize him in his uniform, but it was definitely the same man. "Didn't I see you at—"

"Are you the one who found the body?" he interrupted, ignoring her question. "I need to take down your statement."

Her questions would have to wait for another time. "Yes... I tripped over the body when I was walking towards the road," said Patricia. "I was going to check out an odd noise."

"What did you hear?" asked Brian.

"I heard someone running away," said Patricia. "I called out, but no one answered."

"So you walked towards the sound of the footsteps?" asked Brian.

"Yes," said Patricia. "I wish I had stayed put and called the park ranger instead."

"Perhaps," he said. "Don't beat yourself up about it. This is going to take a bit—you should wait at your RV. The coroner and the forensic team should be here soon."

Patricia stood by her RV with Tom and Valerie, but she

could not seem to go inside. She sat in her camp chair, still in shock, and watched everything. There was a small crowd forming beyond the park rangers blocking the road. Officer Johnson unspooled yellow tape around the crime scene, tying it to the nearby trees. The forensic team arrived and set up lights around the body. The coroner and an ambulance arrived not long after that.

The shock was wearing off, and Patricia felt weak. Tom offered her more tea.

"Thank you, Tom. You and Valerie should go back to your RV. The police are here now. I am sure whoever did this is long gone," said Patricia. Tom agreed with a worried look at Valerie's pale face. He walked back with his wife.

Patricia sipped her tea and waited while the forensic team did their work. Some were taking pictures and others were bagging evidence. Officer Johnson kept glancing over at her as he spoke to the coroner. Patricia stayed outside her RV, guessing that Brian had more questions for her. After about an hour, the ambulance took the body away and the forensic team packed up their equipment. Patricia sat up straighter as Brian walked over.

"You could have waited in your RV," said Brian. "You didn't have to watch all that."

"I don't mind," said Patricia. "I used to work at a police station."

"Oh?" said Brian, intrigued. "What did you do?"

"I was a clerk at first in the records department, but I worked my way up. I helped process evidence and crime reports with the detective unit," said Patricia.

"What do you do now?" Brian kept his attention on her as she spoke, and she was comforted by his solid, calm presence.

"I am a travel writer," said Patricia. "My publisher sends me around the country and I write about different cities and tourist events," Patricia explained. "I live in my RV and drive all over the country."

He nodded, then flipped open his notepad. "Well, I have to ask you a few detailed questions. Did you know the deceased?"

"No, I have never seen him before," said Patricia. "I take walks around the park twice a day, but I have never seen him."

Brian asked her more details about where she had been that evening with Tom and Valerie and what time they had returned.

"Would you like to sit down and have some tea?" asked Patricia.

"No, thank you, ma'am," replied Brian. "I just have a couple more questions and I will be out of your hair." There was a short pause while he wrote down more notes.

"Did you know the deceased?" asked Patricia. Brian looked up and scowled for a moment, and then his face went neutral.

"Even if I did, I cannot tell you that," said Brian. "This is an active police investigation."

"I am aware of that," said Patricia. "I was just making conversation."

Brian shifted his weight and went on with his questions. "When did your neighbor come over?" asked Brian.

"I screamed, and Tom came over and helped me up. His wife Valerie called 911," said Patricia.

Brian checked his watch and sighed. Patricia guessed it must be nearing 4 am, and the sky was beginning to turn blue. Dawn was not too far away. "Do you have a contact number for your friends? I may call them later for follow-up questions," said Brian.

Patricia gave him cell phone numbers for Tom and Valerie and her own number as well. As he stood to go, she hesitated, then asked a question that had been nagging her all night. "Do you think the killer will come back? Could it be someone hiding in the woods around here?"

He shook his head. "I highly doubt that. The forensic team —" he stopped. "Sorry, I can't share any details."

"I noticed that the body was dragged from the road," Patricia commented.

Brian did not reply. He merely pulled out a business card and gave it to Patricia. "There will be officers patrolling the perimeter of the park the next couple of nights. Rest assured we have the investigation under control. The park guests will be notified if there is a threat to public safety. If you have any other questions, or if you remember anything else, please give me a call."

"But you'll let me know if I can be of any help?" said Patricia. "I helped the department where I worked with solving crimes. I could assist."

"Thank you for your offer, but I don't think I'll be needing any…volunteers," said Brian. He did not look pleased. Those blue eyes of his flashed against the dark sky. Patricia bit her tongue and met his glare with her own brave look until he turned to go. She watched his tall figure walk away. Brian cut the spotlight on the now-empty crime scene and drove off.

Patricia was too antsy to sleep, so she paced back and forth outside her trailer for half an hour, staring at the yellow crime scene tape and watching as dawn slowly crept upon the park. She really wanted to help with the investigation, but Brian had basically blown her off. Patricia could not figure out why it bothered her so much.

Just as dawn broke over the park, Patricia felt fatigue overtake her confusion and adrenaline, and she went into her RV. She closed the curtains tight against the light and curled up in her bed. After a little while, she fell into a fitful sleep.

# chapter four

When Patricia woke up, it was after noon and she felt disoriented. She had not slept well. Visions of the dead man had haunted her dreams. When she got up, she brewed herself some coffee. She sat in her RV and sipped her drink until she felt her nerves steady. Last night had been dreadful. Between finding the body and being blown off by the detective, Patricia felt down. She took a deep breath and opened her RV door. The police tape was still around the crime scene, and Patricia was startled to see how close the body had actually been to her RV. At night, distances can be deceiving; Patricia thought she had walked almost up to the road before finding the body. It turns out that the body was only about thirty feet from her RV door.

Patricia wondered if she had startled someone in the act when she came home. She shivered at the thought that the murderer could have been that close to her last night. Patricia shook her head and went back to change and put on her walking shoes. Murder or no, she had to keep working on her article.

However, instead of going to the bus stop to head to another tourist site, Patricia decided to walk around the park. Maybe it would help steady her nerves. Not wanting to disturb her neighbors, she set off on a walking trail in the opposite direction as Tom and Valerie's RV spot. Patricia figured they were still asleep after last night's events. Patricia set out around the park and said hello to some other families and travelers enjoying the natural beauty of the park. It did her good to be reminded that life goes on, despite the shocking things that can happen in the night.

While she was walking, Patricia thought about her strange interaction with Detective Johnson. Did he have something to hide? She did not want to miss the opportunity to be helpful, but perhaps it was simply that police work in Atlanta was a lot different from her small hometown. The mystery of it all nagged at her. *I wonder what happened to that poor victim,* Patricia thought as she rounded the trail to Tom and Valerie's RV.

Tom was sitting outside with a cup of coffee in his hand. Patricia said hello, and Tom looked up with dark circles under his eyes. Patricia guessed hers would match his. Tom told her to sit down. He said in a quiet voice that Valerie was still asleep.

"I am glad one of us is getting some sleep," said Patricia.

"I could not even think of sleeping until everyone left. Even then it was difficult," Tom said, shaking his head. "Would you like some coffee?"

"No, thank you," said Patricia. "I had some a little while ago. I just came by to check on you two."

"Thanks," said Tom. "I let Valerie sleep in…this is not what I had planned for our honeymoon. I just hope she is okay. She looked as pale as a ghost last night."

"Don't worry. A little sleep will bring the color back to her cheeks," said Patricia.

Just then, Valerie stepped out of the RV, dressed and looking refreshed. Tom looked up at her, surprised and happy to see her looking so well. He gave her a hug.

"You know what will really help me recover? A little retail

therapy," Valerie joked. They all laughed. It gave Patricia an idea.

"You know, I do have a mall on my list of attractions to review for this article. Want to come with me for a girls' day of shopping, Val?"

Valerie lit up at this proposal and ran to grab Tom's keys before he could even say anything. He chuckled fondly at his pretty wife. She embraced him and said, "While we're gone, this is your chance. Get a nice, long nap to make up for last night. I'll be in even better spirits after I find a few pretty things to wear for our next dinner out." Patricia fetched her purse too, and then the two women drove off in Tom and Valerie's car. Tom yawned as he waved goodbye to them from the door of the couples' RV.

On the way into town, Patricia and Valerie chatted about everything except what had happened the night before. Instead, they admired the skyline. It was a beautiful day, and the sun shone off the tall downtown buildings as Atlanta came into view.

The downtown mall was large and three stories high. There were three high-end department stores anchoring the major storefronts and a plethora of smaller shops and boutiques. Patricia and Valerie rode the escalators up to the top, admiring the sunny, glassed-in view. They went into the first large store. Patricia tried on a few tops and did not find anything worth buying, but Valerie snagged a flowing gauze skirt on sale, perfect for beach destinations.

The two women chatted as they shopped. The soothing music and background sounds at the mall helped Patricia to get her mind off of what had happened. *There's nothing quite like retail therapy,* thought Patricia. At one boutique she found a dress that fit her like a dream, and when she balked at the price, Valerie exclaimed it was too perfect to pass up. Patricia was grateful for her new friend's comforting presence.

With a few parcels in hand, Valerie stopped to look at a

map. "Let's get some late lunch." Patricia realized her stomach was growling. They found a tavern in the mall and ducked in. There were signature cocktails and a pastrami appetizer that they enjoyed immensely. After their lunch, both Patricia and Valerie seemed to feel a lull in their energy. Valerie turned to Patricia with a kind and sympathetic look.

"Do you want to talk about it?"

Patricia felt bad for her young friend. "I don't want to burden you."

"I'm not a fragile flower, no matter what Tom thinks," Valerie said with a wry grin. "I can tell something more than the murder is weighing on your mind. You'll feel better if you talk about it."

Taking a deep breath, Patricia finally told her about seeing the man from the farmer's market at the Botanical Gardens, and her realization when Detective Brian Johnson came to investigate the scene of the crime. Valerie listened attentively. Patricia sighed. "He ignored my question when I tried to ask if he recognized me. He also blew me off and implied I was trying to get involved where I don't belong."

Valerie frowned. "You were just trying to be helpful. At the very least, he owes you an explanation. Not to mention an apology for what happened at the market. More importantly…he should have answered your first question about why he bumped into you twice in one day." Valerie paused, thinking. "I suppose you were a witness to a major crime, and he had to focus on that."

Patricia wiped the corner of her eyes as a few tears threatened to spill out. "You're right. I just can't seem to let it go." Valerie gave her a quick hug and a reassuring smile.

"I don't want you to worry more than you have to, Patricia. Tom says we should stay out of it. But…you can at least call the detective and get an explanation. Maybe that will help you put this whole episode behind you."

As they paid for lunch and strolled out to the parking lot

to find the car, Patricia felt reassured. She was glad for Valerie's support. She knew exactly what she needed to do when they returned to the Stone Mountain campground. However, she needed more than an apology, no matter what Valerie said. There was something bothering her about the crime scene, and she needed answers.

Patricia looked at the business card that Detective Johnson had given her. The precinct station intimidated her a little bit, but she was determined to get answers. She put the card back in her pocket, entered and greeted a middle-aged woman at the reception desk.

"May I help you?" asked the woman.

"Hello, my name is Patricia, and I am looking for Detective Brian Johnson," said Patricia.

The receptionist buzzed the officer to let him know he had a visitor, then stood to escort Patricia to his office. "He is just down the hall. Right this way, please," the receptionist said.

She followed the receptionist down the hall to a very small and cramped office. The receptionist knocked on the open door.

"Brian, this young lady is here to see you," said the receptionist. Brian Johnson looked up from his desk, eyes wide with surprise. He thanked the receptionist and motioned Patricia to a seat across the desk. Patricia knocked her knee painfully on the desk as she sat down. Brian cleared his throat and apologized for the size of the office.

"I have only been a detective for about three years now. I hope to be promoted so I can get a larger office soon. Can I get you some water or coffee?" Brian asked Patricia. He seemed a little nervous.

"No, thank you," said Patricia. "I'm fine."

"I take it you have more details to add to your statement?"

asked Brian, smoothing his unruly brown hair back from his forehead.

"Not exactly. I was wondering what your forensic team found out about the drag marks," said Patricia. Brian looked taken aback. "I'm still really worried about whether the killer will strike again from the woods near my campsite." His smile faded as she said this.

"I thought we discussed this. There is no ongoing danger. And there were no drag marks," said Brian, his tone short. Patricia gaped.

"What do you mean there were no drag marks?" she asked.

Brian leaned as far back as he could in his chair and looked at her speculatively. "The forensic report came back and there were no drag marks listed. Hence, no drag marks," Brian retorted. He had not expected her to be quite this stubborn. He rested his hands behind his neck.

"But I saw them myself," Patricia insisted.

"Are you saying you trespassed in my crime scene?" asked Brian, his eyebrows raising. He was no longer tilted back. He had his hands on his desk and he was looking straight at Patricia. She sighed.

"No, I mean the night I found the body. The drag marks were plainly visible around the victim's feet." She disliked the look of annoyance that seemed to creep over the detective's features again. "Listen, I told you I have been to plenty of crime scenes, back when I worked for a small police department," Patricia said. "I know what drag marks look like," she insisted, but Brian shook his head dismissively. It infuriated her. "I'll go back and take pictures if you like—"

"You know, I could have you detained for interfering with a criminal case," he interrupted her. Patricia just scoffed.

"What good would that do you? Considering your forensic team, I would be surprised if you could find the correct paperwork to fill out regarding my arrest," said

Patricia, flipping her red curls over her shoulder. Brian stared at her and then shook his head again.

"If you do not have anything new to tell me, I have to get back to work. Stay out of my crime scene. I don't have time for this," Brian said, turning to his computer.

"You will not solve this crime if you do not listen to me," Patricia said, banging her hand on his desk. Patricia was frustrated. She knew what she had seen. She just had to get Brian to believe it. She was desperate. "I'll prove it."

"Pardon me?"

"If you don't want me to go and take pictures, then let's go to the crime scene and I'll show you what I saw. If I'm wrong, I promise I won't bother you again. But if I'm right—"

"If you're right, this investigation has bigger problems than paperwork," Brian mused, thinking about it. "Look. How did you get to my precinct?" Brian asked after a moment.

"I took the bus. Why?" asked Patricia.

"Well, it is almost time for my dinner break. If it will get you off my back, I can drive you back to your RV and you can show me these supposed drag marks," Brian said. Patricia beamed.

"That would make me very happy," she said.

"And when we do not find them, you will leave me alone?" Brian prompted her. "And you will not touch my crime scene?"

"Promise. But when we do find them, you will see that I am right," said Patricia. Brian rolled his eyes, but now he looked more amused than annoyed. He stood up and gestured for her to follow him to the parking lot. Patricia felt butterflies in her stomach, and she hoped it was just her nerves. Brian held open the passenger door of his truck, and she felt the warmth of his hand on her lower back as the handsome detective steadied her. *Okay, maybe more than just nerves.*

She took a breath to steady herself. *I hope I'm right,* Patricia thought, crossing her fingers for luck as they drove down the highway to Stone Mountain.

Brian got them to the campground in record time. He drove the truck to Patricia's RV. They passed Tom and Valerie's RV, and Patricia saw they were gone. She breathed a sigh of relief. She did not want Valerie to know she had gone to see the detective after her advice to stay out of it and simply make a phone call.

Brian pulled up to Patricia's RV, and Patricia hopped out of the truck. She ducked under the police tape before Brian could stop her.

"It's over here," Patricia called over her shoulder.

"At least you know how to walk a crime scene," Brian admitted.

"I told you I have been to a few before," said Patricia. She walked to where the corpse had been lying in the grass and pointed.

"See, they end right there," said Patricia. Brian leaned over. He shook his head. Patricia worried that she might have been wrong and that the grass was like that naturally.

"Well, I'll be darned," said Brian. Patricia smiled. She knew she had been correct. Brian followed the marks to the bushes at the edge of the road and then back to the spot where the body had been discovered.

"Okay, so you were right," said Brian. He put his hands on his hips and examined the scene again.

"So, do you think the killer will come after someone else in the campground?" asked Patricia.

"No," he replied, finally turning to look at her. He cocked his head to the side as if thinking about something. "If I tell you why, will you promise not to spread it around to the press?"

"Scout's honor," said Patricia. She could hear another RV driving slowly down the park road, and nearby some children were riding their bikes on a trail. "How about we go inside first, though?" He nodded, and they exited the crime scene tape and walked over to her RV.

Inside, it was cool and quiet. She offered him a seat at the kitchen table and poured them both a glass of iced tea. He took a long drink and gazed at her with those piercing blue eyes again. Instead of explaining his thinking about the killer's motive, he asked her seriously, "I know it's difficult to think about it, but what do you remember about the body?"

Patricia pictured the cold, still limbs of the man lying in the dark, dewy grass. She shuddered. All had been dark—except for one thing. "His shoes," she blurted out, and Brian nodded. "He was wearing very polished, shiny shoes. Loafers. Not the kind of thing you wear to go camping."

"Exactly."

"That, plus the drag marks tells us he was dumped here from somewhere else, right?"

"Possibly." He looked at her closely. "I'm impressed. How did you end up working at a police department, again?" he asked.

Patricia was gratified that he was not dismissing her out of hand. She offered to make some sandwiches, remembering it was his dinner hour, after all. He agreed, and while she prepared their plates in the kitchen, Patricia told Brian that she had a degree in English and psychology. The police department had hired her to help write up reports and process records. She had picked up details about crime solving from the officers she worked with and started writing crime novels to pass the time. After a while, she was promoted to a better position with the detective division, where she began to help out at crime scenes when they were short-staffed.

"Almost like you were practically an unofficial investigator for the department," he commented. "Why did you leave? Sounds like you were quite good at it."

"Well, I was offered this travel writing gig. I jumped on it, and here I am," said Patricia. It was almost the truth. She did not want to tell him the more painful reasons for her departure.

"So, what do you think?" asked Patricia.

"About what?" teased Brian.

"About me helping you out," said Patricia. Brian smiled.

"Well, considering the fact that my forensic team missed the drag marks, you are in," said Brian. Patricia cheered. "However, I need you to keep quiet about your involvement. As far as anyone else is concerned, you are just a witness. I do not want you to get into any trouble," said Brian.

"I completely understand," said Patricia. "I will keep this on the down low." Brian smiled again. "Listen, Brian. I have a question I've been wanting to ask you—" she started to ask.

Just then, Tom appeared at the open door of her RV and gave a friendly wave. "Hey Patricia, I saw the detective's truck in your driveway. Is everything okay?" asked Tom. "Hello, Officer Johnson."

"Hi Tom. Yes," she said. "Everything is fine. He came to look at the crime scene again and we got to talking."

"Well, I have to get back to my office," said Brian. "I will let you know if anything else comes up." He gave her a meaningful look as if to say, *We will finish this conversation later*.

"Thank you, Detective," said Patricia. Once again, her question about seeing him twice had not been answered. Brian got into his truck and backed out of the lot.

"So, will you be helping him?" asked Tom.

"No," Patricia lied. She did not like lying to Tom, but she had promised Brian that she would keep their working relationship a secret.

"Well, that's too bad," said Tom. "I bet you make a great detective."

"Thank you," said Patricia, feeling guilty. It was getting near the end of the day by now.

"How about you join me and Valerie for some after-dinner wine?" Tom offered. "We were just setting up the fire pit."

"Sounds good," Patricia said. She felt better after a glass of wine. Tom told more stories about their honeymoon travels and they relaxed around the fire. In quiet moments, Patricia found herself thinking more about the case. She was actually looking forward to spending time with Brian. Once he had gotten his stubborn streak out of the way, he turned out to be a really nice guy. Maybe she would be able to tell Tom and Valerie some time down the road.

Valerie leaned over to refill her glass with sparkling rosé wine that smelled like peaches. "I heard the detective stopped by. Did he apologize finally?"

Patricia was flustered. "Well…no, but he did explain some things." She hurriedly asked the couple if they were planning to go to see any more live music events, burying her feelings of guilt. For now, everything would definitely remain a secret between her and Brian. Her attempt at concealment did have one drawback, however. Valerie was too quick for Patricia. She teased Patricia that she was blushing every time Brian was mentioned. Patricia had to admit to herself that she wasn't sure if it was excitement about the investigation or the idea of spending time with the handsome detective that made nervous butterflies flit around in her stomach.

At the end of the night, Tom offered to walk her back to her RV so she would not have to walk alone in the dark. He waited outside the door until she firmly locked and secured it, then waved goodnight and walked back to the couples' campsite. Patricia got ready for bed. Tomorrow she needed to visit a few important cultural stops in Atlanta for her article, but more importantly, getting away from the campground would give her the opportunity to meet up with Brian and finally get some answers and help with the investigation.

Before she turned out the light, she heard her mobile phone buzz. When she picked it up, a text message from Brian glowed in the darkness: *Meet me at the Flying Biscuit tomorrow, 12pm? We have lots to discuss.* Patricia giggled at the name of the restaurant. It rang a bell in her memory, though. When she looked it up on her map, she realized it was not too far from a modern art museum she planned to visit the next day. *Perfect. See you then,* she replied.

Anticipation lingered despite her tiredness, and long after she lay down in bed that night, she stared at the starry skies through the moonroof of her RV, lost in thought.

# chapter five

Patricia hopped on a bus to midtown Atlanta and the art museums early the next morning. Patricia arrived first at the Millennium Gate Museum, dedicated to Georgia state history and culture, and wandered the exhibits for an hour. In the lobby, she picked up a free map to Atlanta cultural destinations. A few places intrigued her. On the spur of the moment, she decided to head to the Margaret Mitchell house, where *Gone with the Wind* was written. Patricia was fascinated by the historical décor and loved seeing the author's writing desk. She felt a kind of kinship with other authors, even if she had an RV instead of a grand house and a laptop instead of a typewriter.

She stepped out onto the sidewalk just in time to catch the MARTA bus to the High Museum of Art. She checked her watch and saw that she still had a while before she was due to meet Brian for lunch.

When she arrived at the museum, Patricia saw that there was an exhibit set up outside the front entrance. It was a bright, modernist playscape, and children were encouraged to climb on the structure. Patricia delighted to see children happily engaged with art. She went inside the sleek, modern museum and wandered through the light-filled galleries.

One of the main exhibitions displayed a variety of modernist sculptures. There were large cubes and intricate designs with lace, strings, cups, and other found objects. It was the first week of the exhibition, so the museum was a bit crowded. The layout allowed people to observe the art close up or at a distance. Patricia was looking at one of the more intricate works when she overheard two people talking in a hush just behind her. It was an older woman and a younger man.

"Can you believe he's gone?" the older woman asked the younger man.

"I know. It is such a shock to the community. And way out in the woods? How could this have happened?" the younger man replied. Both were dressed very smartly, and the woman was dripping in diamonds. She shook her head and clucked her tongue in disapproval.

"It is such a shame. Wasn't he about to open his new club next month?" she asked the young man.

"Yes. I heard those old rumors going around again, though…" he said, his voice dropping to an even quieter tone. Patricia held absolutely still so she could overhear every word.

"Oh really?" asked the older woman. "That surprises me. I thought he had put all that behind him."

"Imperial Capital Bank did not want to make the same mistake twice," said the young man. "Perhaps he…you know…" He made a motion by his head as if to indicate Peter Sedgewick had killed himself. The older woman gasped in horror at this suggestion and shook her head vehemently.

"Surely not. I have it on good authority that they are investigating it as a murder," she said with finality. The conversation devolved into whispers, and soon Patricia could not hear anything.

By the time she turned carefully to look, the older woman and the young man had strolled off into the crowd. Patricia grabbed her phone and went out into the hallway to call Brian.

The phone rang, and the receptionist answered. She put Patricia's call through to Brian.

"Good morning," said Brian.

"Hello," said Patricia excitedly. "I am at the museum, and I overheard a conversation. Listen, you're going to have more rumors on your hands if you don't get this investigation moving soon."

She heard his dissatisfied mutter in the background. "What was the conversation?" asked Brian.

"A rich woman and man were talking about a certain murder. It seems like the person who was murdered was an up-and-coming businessman. Is that our guy?" asked Patricia.

"Wow, word travels fast. Yes. But that's not privileged information, the press already knew about that."

"Did the press write that he may have offed himself over a bad business deal? That's what the young man was saying." Patricia thought she heard him swear softly into the phone.

"I would rather not go into this over the phone. I know it's a little early, but can you meet me at the restaurant in ten minutes?" Brian asked Patricia.

"Sure," said Patricia. She hung up the phone, her heart beating in her chest. On her way out, she looked for the two people she had heard talking but saw no one she recognized. Outside in the bright spring sunshine, Patricia hailed a cab to the restaurant, feeling like she was finally proving her worth on this investigation.

At the Flying Biscuit, Patricia settled into a quiet booth to wait for Brian and asked the waitress to leave them a carafe of coffee. She suspected they would need the energy, and when Brian arrived, her hunch proved correct. He arrived with a sheaf of files. After the waitress stopped by to take their orders, they sipped their coffee.

"Were you out enjoying Atlanta before you called?" Brian asked.

"Yes. It's a fun city," said Patricia. "At least, most of it is."

"It is a great town," said Brian. "I am just sorry you had to see this side of it."

"I don't mind," said Patricia, remembering how fiercely she had wished for a chance to get back into detective work.

"Did you enjoy the museum?" Brian asked.

"I did," said Patricia.

"I enjoy the modernists, but my real passion is post-impressionism," said Brian. Patricia could not help the surprise from crossing her face.

"What? A detective cannot study art?" asked Brian, smiling.

"Well, no, but the ones I worked with would not know the difference between a Matisse and a Picasso," Patricia replied.

"I went to the big university in Athens. Everyone ends up taking some form of art appreciation. Athens has a huge music scene, too. It has been the birthplace of many up-and-coming bands," Brian explained.

"I am familiar with the scene out of Athens," said Patricia with a smile. "I had hoped to add Athens to this trip, actually, but I think my publisher is going to send me somewhere else soon."

"That's too bad. I'd be happy to show you around Athens any day. Any ideas where you're headed next?" asked Brian.

"Not really," said Patricia. "But enough about my travel plans. What can you tell me about our victim?"

"Okay, back to work," Brian smiled. "Our victim was Peter Sedgewick. Early forties, married, no criminal record. He was a successful businessman. He was set to open a club in Buckhead next month. According to the grapevine, he is Atlanta's next big thing. At least, he was until he was found dead."

"Do we have any idea how he got to the campground?" asked Patricia.

"I have no idea. He had on an Armani suit in addition to those Brooks Brothers loafers you noticed," he said.

"Those are definitely not camping shoes," Patricia agreed.

"Tell me exactly what you overheard at the museum," Brian asked. She told him about the conversation and especially the detail about old rumors and Imperial Capital Bank.

"The young man said the bank would not 'make the same mistake twice'...what do you think he meant by that?" Patricia asked.

"I am not sure. I am lining up some people to interview. Would you like to come along with me when I question them?" asked Brian. "We can ask about the bank matter as well as everything else. I can use all the help I can get in this case. If I break this case, I could be up for promotion. If I lose it, I could be a beat cop patrolling the street again next month."

"I would be happy to help," said Patricia happily. She did not tell Brian she had never questioned anyone before. That was information he did not need to know. The waitress brought their food—a potato scramble for Patricia, and a sausage and biscuit with gravy platter for Brian—and they ate while they talked.

"I will probably be doing most of the talking during the interviews," said Brian. "However, if you observe the people and their surroundings, we can check in after each interview and see if I missed anything."

"Sounds great," said Patricia. "When do we start?"

Brian was distracted for a moment by his mobile phone beeping at him, and he checked a message on it. "Well, I was hoping to start today, but most people cannot meet me until tomorrow," said Brian. "Besides, my chief just emailed me. I have a few other investigative leads I have to cross off my list this afternoon before we can head to the interviews tomorrow. Listen…I have to head back for a meeting."

Patricia was disappointed. They had only been talking for about ten minutes. "We did not even get a chance to review the files you brought."

"I'm sorry," he said. "Can I make it up to you over dinner? We can go down the list of suspects, and I can tell you the background on everybody. I know you've got lots of research for your article to do, though. Maybe you don't have enough time…"

"Well," said Patricia, eager to find a way to make it work, "only if it's someplace I can add to my article about Atlanta. Do you have any good ideas?"

He nodded. "There is this bar in Little Five Points. It has a good variety of beer and a great menu, all local and organic," said Brian. "I could pick you up at the campground and take you there if you want."

"That will work," said Patricia. She was happy to have dinner with Brian. She was enjoying his company.

"Okay. I will pick you up around six," Brian said. He paid the bill and tossed her a cheeky grin on his way out. "Dress nice tonight. It's a fancy place."

"I look forward to it," Patricia said with a smile. Patricia watched Brian saunter down the sidewalk. *Is this just another meeting, or is he taking me on a date tonight?* she wondered, confused but excited. Just then, her phone rang.

"Hello?" said Patricia.

"Hello, Patricia, this is Lenore," said the familiar voice of her editor and publisher on the other end of the line.

"Hello, Lenore," said Patricia. "How are you?"

"I am cold. It is snowing up here. Can you believe that?" the older woman responded. She lived in Chicago. Patricia was not surprised that it was still snowing there.

"I appreciate you sending me somewhere warm," said Patricia.

"You're welcome. How is the article coming?" asked Lenore.

"It is coming along well," said Patricia.

"Will you be done soon?" asked Lenore.

"I plan to be, why?" asked Patricia. She wondered if she should tell Lenore about the body that had been discovered outside her RV but decided not to chance it.

"I have confirmed your next assignment. When I tell you, you will flip," said Lenore with a delighted cackle of laughter. Patricia's interest was piqued.

"So, where are you sending me?" she asked.

"Are you sitting down?" asked Lenore.

"Yes," Patricia laughed. "Now tell me the destination."

"Paris," said Lenore.

"What? Wait. You mean Paris, Texas, right?" asked Patricia. Lenore had made this joke before. Patricia had learned the hard way that Rome was also the name of a village in rural Ohio.

"No, Patricia. I mean Paris, France," said Lenore. Patricia could not believe her ears. She had been waiting for an overseas trip for a while. Paris was a dream come true. But Patricia was torn. She had told Brian she would help him with his investigation.

"How soon do you need me there?" asked Patricia, stalling.

"As soon as you wrap up Atlanta," said Lenore. "What are you waiting for? I thought you'd be hopping on the next flight."

"I have to figure out where to store my RV, for one thing. Give me a few days to process this news and make some plans and I'll call you back, okay?" asked Patricia. Patricia figured she could stall for time and try to help Brian with the case.

"Okay, but don't take too long. Paris is calling," said Lenore.

"Thank you, Lenore. I'm so excited! Talk to you soon," Patricia said and hung up. She got up from the table and tried to sort out her thoughts. She was almost done writing her article about Atlanta, but she wanted to see the investigation through. Not to mention she was enjoying her time with Brian immensely. *At least I will be able to sit in on the interviews tomorrow,* Patricia thought while walking outside the restaurant. *Not to mention I'll be seeing him tonight.*

Patricia hopped a bus and rode a little ways uptown to the Center for Puppetry Arts, a museum and theatre that had drawn Patricia's attention. It was not just for children, and Patricia was intrigued. She went inside and viewed the fascinating display of puppets from around the world and from famous movies and television shows. There was a puppet-making class for children and children's puppetry shows all afternoon. They also had a show aimed at teens and adults that was about to start, so Patricia bought a ticket and found her seat. It was an interesting show with no cute puppets, just intricate, experimental forms in dark colors with somber lighting, and the performance left her in a contemplative mood. Patricia clapped loudly at the end.

In the bus on the way back to the campground, Patricia watched the beautiful green trees speed past her window and tried to quiet the butterflies swarming in her stomach as she thought forward to her dinner with Brian that night.

# chapter six

Patricia got ready for dinner and tried to remind herself that this was, after all, more research for her article. She would have another chic restaurant to add to her write-up. She put on a new skirt she had picked up at the mall and her favorite spring top. Usually she did not wear much makeup, but for tonight she put on a bit more. She was just putting on her lipstick when she heard a truck pull up to the RV. She quickly grabbed her purse and went out the RV door. Brian was just getting out of his truck.

"You look great," he said as he walked over. Patricia felt herself blush.

"Thank you," she replied. She locked the door to her RV and Brian opened the door of his truck and Patricia hopped in. Thankfully, Tom and Valerie were not around just then and so did not see her driving by with the detective.

They drove through congested Atlanta traffic until they were near Little Five Points. The traffic opened up, and they got a parking space near the bar. Patricia was impressed. She teased him that he had called ahead and used his status as an officer of the law to get preferential treatment.

"Never!" laughed Brian. "You're just my lucky charm," he joked back.

"You're the charmer," said Patricia. They were both laughing, and she saw that his blue eyes were warm when they looked at her. That certainly didn't help her butterflies.

Brian led her to the restaurant and opened the door. Patricia walked in and admired the cozy décor. Brian signaled the hostess for a table for two and they followed the hostess past the long bar and up some steps to the tables. It was a quiet, intimate restaurant, with little candles in jars on each table. Suddenly it felt even more like a date. Was she imagining things? Patricia tried to put it out of her mind and concentrated on her beautiful surroundings.

Old wine casks and bottles lined the walls and soft, jazzy blues guitar played in the background. Ornate ceiling fans spun lazily, and their water was served in pretty mason jars. Brian ordered a beer, and Patricia took her time with the drink menu. Brian had been right. There were six pages of drinks, including a whole section for beers on tap. Patricia scanned the menu and finally chose a local craft brew.

"So tell me about the interviews. Who are we meeting and what time do we start?" asked Patricia.

"We are scheduled to meet Peter Sedgewick's wife Hannah at ten in the morning. I can pick you up at nine," said Brian.

"That works for me," said Patricia. "Does he have—uh, did he—that is…"

"Do they have any children?" he supplied helpfully. She nodded. "No children. He worked a lot, from what I can tell. He and his wife were quite the power couple in Atlanta society. I spent yesterday afternoon tracking down his mobile phone records, but they weren't much help. We already knew his cell phone wasn't with him in the woods, so it did not explain how he got there."

"Do you suspect his wife had something to do with his death?"

"Well, the family is where we always start. I'm more

interested in his business dealings now, especially with what you overheard at the museum. You really are my lucky charm, you know—you just happened to be in the right place at the right time to overhear that conversation."

Patricia felt herself blush a little again. "I'm just glad you're letting me help out." The waitress brought their drink orders just then. Brian held up his glass towards her.

"To my lucky charm," he said with a smile. Their glasses clinked together, and she took a first sip of her cold, citrusy beer. She found she did not know where to look when his piercing blue eyes looked at her like that. Patricia was grateful when the waitress came back to take their dinner order.

"Now that business is out of the way, where are you originally from?" asked Brian.

"I am from Eastern Pennsylvania," said Patricia. "I went to a big university there, and after graduation I ended up working for the local police department, as I said before."

"And that is where you got your inspiration to write mystery novels," said Brian.

"That is correct," said Patricia. "Working there helped me get the correct lingo."

"I see," said Brian. "So, did you really investigate a Coal Mine Killer in your town?" Patricia blushed again. She was proud of her writing, but she had not expected him to know anything about it.

"Did you read my book? Oh, goodness. No, of course not. I would never use details from a real case in my writing."

"It was a good read. Very realistic."

"Thanks. What about you? Where are you from?" asked Patricia, deliberately changing the subject.

"A small town about fifty miles south of here," said Brian. "I was born and raised there."

"What made a small-town boy move to the big city?" asked Patricia.

"Well, when I was in Athens, my buddies and I used to come to Atlanta for the weekend. Baseball games, college football, concerts. I loved the city. I applied to departments here as soon as I graduated with my criminal justice degree. I was hired here and worked my way up to detective," Brian answered.

"That is impressive," said Patricia.

"So where else have you been?" asked Brian.

"Do you mean in the country?" Patricia asked.

"We can start with Atlanta," said Brian. Patricia smiled. She worked backwards from that day's explorations, starting with the museums and historical sites and going back to the attractions at Stone Mountain from the first day of her visit. She hesitated and did not continue to the part about the Botanical Garden and the Dekalb Farmer's Market.

"Aside from that night at the campground, you've felt safe in Atlanta? You must be used to it, traveling alone," he said.

"I have a gypsy soul," she laughed. "I'm used to fending for myself." She looked up at him and thought, *Now's my chance*. "There was this one guy, though…"

Brian sat up and frowned. "Tell me. Do you need to file a report?"

"I don't know. He was so rude to me in the farmer's market, and then I saw him again in the Botanical Garden. I'm pretty sure he's a pickpocket, though maybe I'm jumping to conclusions. Never judge a book by its cover, I say," she said.

Brian laughed, a deep chuckle that rumbled through him and made his eyes crinkle up at the edges in a way she found very adorable. "I was wondering when I would have to explain that. There were reports of a pickpocket ring operating at tourist locations around the city. I was working undercover," he explained.

"That explains why you didn't just explain that you were a cop. I can't believe you thought I was just some hapless tourist about to get robbed," Patricia said, laughing along with him. She felt better now that the misunderstanding was cleared up.

"When I saw you at the Atlanta Botanical Garden, I thought maybe you were stalking me," he joked. "I was all over Atlanta gathering intel that day, especially at the parks around town. I have to say, I was a little disappointed when I didn't see you at the Skyview Ferris Wheel."

"That's one place I have not been yet," Patricia said.

"No?" Brian asked. "We will have to fix that." Their dinner came, and they continued their discussion over a delicious meal of seafood risotto for Patricia and steak roulades with roasted sweet potatoes for Brian.

"Where else have you traveled?" Brian asked Patricia. She told him about New York and Las Vegas. Patricia told him it had been snowing in New York City when she left.

"I do not miss that much snow," said Patricia. "I especially do not miss it when I am driving my RV."

"I'm sure. We got one inch of snow here a few years ago and it paralyzed the city," said Brian. "I was up all night trying to get people to get off the freeway. At one point, people were just abandoning their cars."

"They were leaving them on the highway?" Patricia asked. "Didn't they worry that someone would crash into them, or steal them?"

"I guess they figured we would keep an eye on them. I would have rather been at home, but I had to babysit cars. It was awful," said Brian. "Fortunately, no one died from exposure. We had to make sure people were inside for the night."

"I did not think about that. I bet people here do not have good winter coats," said Patricia.

"No, they do not, and it stayed very cold that night," said Brian.

"I am glad no one got hurt," said Patricia.

"The only person who got hurt was some fool who was trying to steal cars. He had borrowed a friend's tow truck and was trying to latch a car to it when the car slipped on the ice and ran over his foot. We found him about half a mile away, limping down the road," said Brian. Patricia stifled a laugh.

"Karma will get you, every time," she said. "Have you travelled anywhere?" Patricia asked Brian.

"I sometimes go down to the Gulf. Some friends of mine have a fishing boat and they invite me to go fishing with them a couple of times a year. That is about as far as I have gone, aside from a school trip to Washington D.C. when I was in high school," said Brian. "I would like to travel, but I just don't have the time right now. Work keeps me busy."

"I imagine so," said Patricia. "I suppose that's one of the reasons why I left the police station. I needed more freedom. Now my work takes me all over the country, and maybe even the world, if I'm lucky. I am never in one place long enough to settle down. I keep some belongings in storage at my parents' house up north. They don't mind, as long as I come back for holidays," she said with a grin. "I suppose that is the closest thing I have to a home base. I love my RV. The whole world is my home."

"That does sound like fun," said Brian. His eyes were far away as if he was imagining trying out her lifestyle. "I enjoy my job, even if it does keep me in Atlanta."

"There are worse places to be stranded," said Patricia, looking into his gorgeous eyes and daring a small, flirtatious smile. Brian grinned back. They had finished their dinner and were sitting at the table. Brian said he wanted to take Patricia somewhere. Would she be willing to go?

"Sure," said Patricia. Brian was a gentleman and fun to be around. Patricia was having a great night. She followed him to his truck. He opened the door for her and then got into the driver's side.

"You really need to see this city from a different view at night," said Brian.

"Okay," said Patricia. They drove for about ten minutes, and Brian parked by some trees in a city park. Patricia hopped out of the truck, and Brian guided her between the trees. They stepped out onto a plaza lit by the colorful lights of the city in the background. In front of them was Atlanta's famous Skyview, the largest Ferris wheel Patricia had ever seen. It was incredible.

"I hope you're not afraid of heights," said Brian.

"Not at all," said Patricia. Brian helped her onto the enclosed capsule after he bought their tickets and they rode up to the top of the wheel. Patricia was in awe of the scenery. The city was all lit up and beautiful. Brian pointed out places of interest to her as they descended. The second time up, the wheel went a bit faster. Patricia gasped and clutched onto Brian's hand. She let go when the ride ended. Brian did not mention the hand holding. Patricia was grateful for his warm, companionable silence as they stepped out of the Ferris wheel compartment.

"I hope you enjoyed the ride," said Brian.

"I did," said Patricia. "Thank you." She and Brian walked around the park together for about half an hour. He told her about the park and the Ferris wheel and Patricia listened to his stories. She was having a wonderful time. She knew deep inside that she could not be in a relationship due to her job, but it was fun to hang out with Brian for the night. She also knew he was devoted to his job, so there was that. Patricia was just happy to be walking around with him. When their walk circled back around near his truck, Brian said he needed to call it a night.

"I agree. I want to be in tip-top shape for tomorrow's questionings," Patricia said. Brian drove her back to her RV and opened the truck door. He walked her to the door of her RV and leaned down to kiss her cheek goodnight.

"I had a great night," said Brian. He looked like he wanted to say something more.

"So did I," said Patricia softly.

He stood up straighter, looking every inch the professional detective. "Well, I'll see you tomorrow morning," he said.

"I'm looking forward to it," said Patricia. She watched him walk to his truck and then waved goodbye. He did not leave until her door was unlocked and she was safely ensconced in her RV.

# chapter seven

Patricia was waiting by her RV the next morning when Brian pulled up in his truck. Just as she was about to get in, Tom appeared.

"Hey Patricia, what's going on?" asked Tom. Patricia hesitated.

"I have some further questions for her," Brian interrupted. "I thought I would drive her to the station so she could avoid the bus."

"Oh, that was thoughtful," said Tom. Patricia breathed a sigh of relief. Not only did she not like lying to Tom, she was not very good at it. Patricia opened the truck door.

"I'll see you later, Tom," she said.

"Okay. Maybe Valerie and I will text you about dinner?" Tom replied.

"That sounds good. I might do some more wandering around after my meeting with the detective," Patricia replied while shutting the truck door. Tom leaned into the window.

"If he gives you any problems, just call me. I will be right there," Tom muttered to Patricia with a look at Brian.

"I am sure I'll be fine," she replied. "Thank you for looking out for me." Patricia smiled at Tom, and he backed away from the truck.

"You have some very protective friends," Brian commented as he pulled away.

"He is just being sweet," said Patricia.

Instead of driving to the station, Patricia and Brian drove to the more wealthy part of town. The houses were more mansion-like, and there were luxury condominiums on almost every street. Patricia whistled.

"These houses are gorgeous," she said.

"The people around here do not spare any expense when it comes to their homes," Brian replied. He pulled into one of the driveways.

"This is Peter Sedgewick's house. His wife said she would be home and available for questions," said Brian.

"This house is huge," said Patricia. The tasteful colonial mansion had towering columns up to the second floor and immaculately groomed gardens.

"Like I said, he was pretty successful at his job," said Brian, getting out of the truck. He opened Patricia's door and the pair walked to the front door. Their knock was answered by a friendly woman in her fifties. She told Brian and Patricia to come inside.

"Who is it, Lilith?" Patricia heard a woman's voice coming from the other room.

"It's the detective, ma'am," Lilith replied. With a start, Patricia realized Lilith was a maid. Lilith led Patricia and Brian to a large, sunny living room. There were two brocade sofas and a grand piano. Art hung on the walls, and Patricia guessed that one or two of the knick-knacks on the coffee table might be worth more than her RV. The shelves on the wall were lined with antique leather-bound books. Even without seeing them up close, Patricia could guess they were rare. A woman in her forties stood up and held out her hand to shake Brian's. She had perfectly coiffed blonde hair, and she was wearing an elegantly tailored black dress.

"You must be Detective Johnson," said the woman.

"Yes, I am. Please, Mrs. Sedgewick, call me Brian," Brian replied.

"Thank you. Please call me Hannah. I am Peter's wife," the woman said. Patricia noted that Hannah still referred to her husband in the present tense.

"This is my assistant, Patricia," Brian said. Hannah shook Patricia's hand. Hannah had an air of sorrow about her. She appeared to be in a somber mood despite her perfect appearance. Diamond studs glittered from her ears. While she was holding herself together, Patricia had the feeling that Brian should go easy or Hannah might start crying. Fortunately, Brian had picked up the same vibe.

"I am so sorry for your loss," he said to Hannah.

"Thank you," she said, sitting back down on the sofa. She motioned to Brian and Patricia to sit on the other sofa. They complied.

"I know this time is difficult for you," Brian continued. "I do have to ask you some questions, though."

"I understand," said Hannah. She pulled a tissue out of a nearby box and dabbed at her eyes.

"Do you know of anyone who would want to hurt Peter?" Brian asked Hannah.

"No. Not really," Hannah replied. "His work can be cutthroat, but I do not think anyone at his company is capable of this…" she trailed off, as if unconvinced.

"Was your husband very competitive?" Brian asked.

"Yes, but so was everyone else in his company. It's just the nature of their work. He was well-liked. He channeled a lot of his extra energy into the club he was working on. He was planning to leave his job soon, you know. My husband planned to strike out on his own when his club took off," Hannah said. She sniffed slightly and blew her nose.

"To your knowledge, there was nothing in the way of the club launching? No financial issues?" Brian asked.

Hannah looked up at the detective, but her face was unreadable. "No, nothing like that."

"Okay," said Brian. "Is there anything else we should know?" Hannah glanced at Patricia and then turned her gaze to Brian. A single tear rolled down her cheek.

"Maybe there was someone at his company who didn't want him to succeed, who didn't want him to strike out on his own. He was having an affair," she said, her voice breaking. Patricia held in the gasp that wanted so desperately to come out. Brian did not even flinch.

"Who was he having an affair with?" asked Brian.

"I am not sure," said Hannah. She dabbed her eyes delicately. "However, I will say this much. Whenever I called his office, that girl always had an excuse for why he couldn't come to the phone."

"Who?" Brian asked.

"That little secretary of his. She was always covering for him. She must have known something all along, but she would never admit it to me on the phone no matter how many times I begged." Hannah Sedgewick looked down in shame, then lifted her head defiantly. "Maybe she's the one who has something to hide."

"That's a very serious accusation. Are you certain?" asked Brian.

"Yes," said Hannah. She said it without flinching.

"Did you ever confront Peter about it?" Brian asked. Patricia admired how his voice remained calm and sympathetic, almost as if he was confiding that he would have liked to confront the man himself, if the rumor were true.

Hannah lost control of her perfect façade and wept into a tissue. At the sound, Lilith appeared in the doorway, a look of concern on her face, but Brian waved her away. Finally, Hannah took a deep breath and looked up, her face calm again. "I did confront him…I told him he had to end it. He said…he said I had nothing to worry about." She stared out the windows.

Patricia imagined Hannah having the conversation with her husband. Patricia bet that Hannah was more unflinching during that conversation.

"Why do you think he said that?" asked Brian.

"Because he knew how high the stakes were," Hannah replied. "With his new club opening coming up, he was going to be even more in the public eye. We both knew something like this could ruin him. I guess I made the mistake of thinking he would be honorable and tell me the truth." There was an edge of bitterness to her voice. "Now I'll never know."

"But you think his secretary does," said Brian. There was a silence in the room, as if Hannah Sedgewick did not wish to acknowledge Brian's statement. Patricia saw only how the young, beautiful widow sat ramrod-straight and looked like the picture of composure once more.

"Did you have any other questions for me?" Hannah asked. "I have to go to the funeral home and make more preparations for Peter's memorial service."

"No, that should be all for now," said Brian. "I will be in touch if I need to question you further."

"I certainly won't be going anywhere," said Hannah smoothly. "Planning a memorial service for a man like my husband is not an easy task. It will be a large affair, and it has taken all my time." Brian and Patricia took this as their cue to stand up. Lilith appeared and walked them to the door.

"Lilith," Brian asked when they were out of earshot from Hannah, "do you know if Mr. Sedgewick was having an affair?"

"I don't know," said Lilith. "I mainly assist Mrs. Sedgewick with the household. I try to stay out of the family's personal lives. It's so tragic…she is such a young widow. They were so in love." Tears formed in Lilith's eyes, and Brian thanked her. He and Patricia walked back to his truck.

"So, what do you think?" asked Patricia. It was sad to see such grief up close. She understood now the challenge of discerning fact from fiction in these interviews.

"Well, I would certainly call jealousy over the affair a good motive," said Brian. "I definitely have Mrs. Sedgewick on the top of my list."

"But what about the secretary? And what if Hannah was wrong about the affair to begin with? I'm not even certain she was telling us the whole story about what she knows."

"Grief can be a funny thing," Brian commented. "Let's not read too much into it just yet. Our next stop will tell us more. We are scheduled to meet a few people at Peter Sedgewick's office." He started the truck and they drove downtown.

Brian parked the truck next to a tall building and came around to open her door. Patricia got out of the truck and looked up. She felt a wave of dizziness and held onto the truck.

"Are you okay?" asked Brian, catching her arm.

"Yes," said Patricia. "I got dizzy looking up." She laughed and let go of the truck but couldn't seem to let go of his arm. Brian led her into the building, only letting go to hold open the door for her. Brian walked up to the large desk on the first floor.

"I am looking for Jeff Jones' office. Peter Sedgewick's partner," Brian told the receptionist.

"Is Mr. Jones expecting you?" the receptionist inquired.

"Yes. My name is Detective Johnson, and this is my assistant," Brian replied as he showed the receptionist his badge.

"Yes, sir," she replied. "His office is on the thirtieth floor."

"Thank you," said Brian. Patricia followed Brian to the elevator. On the way up, Brian hummed along with the piped-in music. Patricia smiled.

"You must be the only person I've met who actually likes

elevator music," Patricia observed. Brian stopped humming and smiled back at Patricia.

"What can I say? I have a thing for eighties music," he replied and then took up his tune again. Patricia smiled, and the elevator glided to a halt on the thirtieth floor. Patricia walked out, and Brian followed her. The elevator opened onto a large, modern reception area with one desk in the center. A pretty young woman was sitting at the desk. An engraved nameplate in front of her computer read *Lana Morris.*

"You must be Detective Johnson," she said with a nod. Patricia noted a few condolence cards lying on her desk.

"Yes. I have an appointment with Jeff Jones. Is he available?" Brian asked.

"Yes, he is. You can go into the hall on the left. His door is the last one down the hallway," said Lana.

"Miss Morris, were you also secretary to Peter Sedgewick?" Brian asked her.

"Yes, I am," she replied. "I am the administrative assistant for Peter and Jeff's division. That is, I was, until…" she trailed off, as if unsure how to say it. Her eyes were rimmed with tears that did not fall.

"Perhaps we can talk after my appointment," said Brian.

Lana nodded. "I will answer anything you need me to," the young woman replied. Tears rolled down her cheek and she grabbed a tissue. "I am sorry. I am just so upset that he is gone."

"I understand," said Brian. "Let me talk to Mr. Jones and I will get back to you."

"Okay," the young woman sniffed.

"I'm so sorry for your loss," Patricia said to her before they moved down the hallway. Brian led the way. Their footsteps were muffled by the carpeting and there was an unusual silence in the hallway. Patricia felt like she was in a vacuum. The last door opened, and a good-looking man in his forties walked out to greet them.

"Detective Johnson?" the man asked while holding out his hand. "Right on time."

"Yes. Are you Mr. Jones?" Brian asked the man.

"I am. Please, call me Jeff. And who might you be?" Mr. Jones asked, eyeing Patricia.

"This is my assistant, Patricia," said Brian.

"Very well, why don't you both come in and sit down," said Mr. Jones. Patricia and Brian followed him into his office. Patricia noticed the large windows and the stunning view. Mr. Jones sat behind his oak desk.

"Please, have a seat," he said.

"Thank you for agreeing to meet today. I know the loss is fresh, and I appreciate your willingness to help. I just have a few questions for you," said Brian.

"Of course," said Jeff. "I am as anxious as you to find out what happened to Peter."

"Tell me more about him. Were you close?" Brian asked.

"I wouldn't say we were best friends, but we have known each other since college. We joined this firm about fifteen years ago and have been in charge of this division for the last six years."

"Do you know of any enemies he may have acquired in his business dealings or his private life?"

"No. Everyone liked Peter. That is why he was able to climb the ladder so quickly. He was just one of those people that everyone wanted to be around. He was always that way," Jeff replied.

"Were you partners in the club venture?" asked Brian.

"No, I am not. He did that all on his own, even though it caused some tension between him and his wife." Jeff hesitated briefly. "This business venture of his has been an all-consuming passion for the last few years. He has certainly had some setbacks with it—everyone knows what happened with the first club—but I'm pretty sure he had worked out the kinks on this plan. He showed me the plans many times," said Jeff. He smiled sadly. "It was going to be a beautiful place. He was probably going to quit this job once the club became successful. He could have done anything in this city, with that kind of success under his belt."

"What's this about a first club?" Brian asked.

"I don't know if it's worth telling about…it was when he was quite young. Just out of college. He was going to open up a club right after he got married to Hannah. He had the finances lined up with Imperial Capital and everything. However, he was a very, very young man, and we all make mistakes." Jeff spread his hands apologetically.

"What do you mean?" asked Patricia.

"All of Atlanta high society knew about it, though you'll never find a word in the papers. His plans fell apart because…well, the stress got to him, and he took his college partying habits a bit too far, let's say. His family sent him to a rehab program for a couple months."

Brian raised his eyebrows at this. "Did he have a substance abuse problem recently?"

Jeff shook his head. "Not after that. I'm sure the autopsy would tell you that much. As far as I know, once he returned from rehab, he swore off the bad stuff and was on the straight and narrow. I was so pleased to get my old friend back, I helped him get the job here, not more than a month after I started. That was almost fifteen years ago."

"So, you don't think stress was weighing him down about the new club," Brian mused. "Do you think the tension with his wife might have to do with a substance abuse problem coming back to haunt him? Or could the tension have caused his substance abuse problem to come back?"

Jeff leaned back in his chair and sighed. "Peter was a smart guy, a driven man. I trusted him. As far as I know, there was nothing like that." He looked weary and sad. "But he didn't tell me everything. I don't know. Hannah would know more about it. Have you spoken to her?"

"We're talking to everyone Peter knew well," Brian replied, avoiding a direct answer. To Patricia's ears, Jeff's words seemed to be revealing a lot. Brian skillfully guided the conversation onward. "Tell me more about your work with him. Did you compete in this job a lot?"

"Sometimes, but it was more of a friendly competition. Peter and I were unofficial partners here. He and I worked together on projects a lot. We knew each other's strengths and used them to move up in the company," said Jeff.

"Were you on the same level in the company?" asked Brian.

"Yes," said Jeff. "At least, until we took charge of this division and Brian got his latest project. But like I said, he could have gone out on his own after the club took off. I probably would have taken over any of the projects he left behind. As it is, I'm working on his project now."

"How does that make you feel?" asked Brian.

"I was happy for his success," said Jeff. "Peter had put his all into this company and into his new venture with the club. I felt he was finally getting what he deserved. Peter and I had talked about going into business together, but I wanted to stay with the company. He was always working a little bit harder than me, pushing a little bit more, but like I said—we all loved him for it."

"He sounds like a good man," said Brian.

"He was," said Jeff. "I never in my life thought I'd be taking up his duties at work because of his death." He said the last word on a quiet note. Brian thanked Jeff for his time. Patricia got up with Brian and they moved toward the door of Jeff's office. Patricia thought perhaps the man wanted to be left alone with his thoughts.

However, at the last moment, Jeff Jones stood with an agitated look and came around to block them from exiting.

"Is there something else, Mr. Jones?" Brian asked.

"Listen, my secretary has been having a very hard time of

it. Lana can be...emotionally volatile. I'm sure there are details you need to get from her about Peter's last few days. Can I ask you to do me a favor? Maybe wait a few more days and she can answer questions over the phone instead?"

Brian and Patricia exchanged a look. Patricia thought it sounded as if Jeff Jones was trying to control Lana's access to the police.

"Mr. Jones, I assure you that I will take every precaution to ensure that our questions for Miss Morris are gentle. However, I'm afraid I must insist that I question her in person, and today," Brian said. Jeff nodded and seemed resigned. He followed them back to the front reception area.

Lana Morris was still sitting at her desk when Brian and Patricia approached. Brian asked if she had some time to talk to them, and she said yes. Jeff hovered in the background fiddling with papers at the copy machine but did not say anything.

"Let me put the phone on auto answer," Lana said. After taking care of the phone, she stood up. She was a young, shapely brunette. She had on a pencil skirt and her linen shirt had the top two buttons unbuttoned.

"Is there a conference room where we can speak?" asked Brian.

"Yes," said Lana. "Just down the hall." She hesitated and grabbed a box of tissues off of her desk. Patricia tried to watch Jeff out of the corner of her eye as they followed Lana down the hall. About halfway down was a conference room. Luckily, there were windows out into the hallway, so Jeff would have no way of lingering there to overhear Lana through the door.

Lana Morris sat down and crossed her long, tanned legs. Patricia noticed she was not wearing nylons with her high heels, but it was a warm day, and this was Georgia after all. Perhaps office attire was a bit different from what she was used to up north. Brian and Patricia sat opposite her.

"What do you need to know?" asked Lana.

"I understand this is a difficult time. We hope that your answers will help us track down some important leads. First off, did Peter have any enemies? Anyone who would want to harm him?" asked Brian.

"Oh no, absolutely not," said Miss Morris. She seemed shocked.

"Are you sure, Miss Morris?" asked Brian.

"Yes. And you can call me Lana," she replied.

"Okay, Lana," Brian continued. "How were his relationships with his coworkers?"

"We all got along really well with him," said Lana. She hesitated, and tears rolled down her cheek. "I am sorry," she said.

"Take your time," Brian coaxed. Lana wiped her eyes and continued.

"I cannot believe he is gone," Lana said. Her eyes welled up again. "He was such a great boss. He was the best, kindest man."

"When was the last time you saw him?" Brian asked.

"I saw him for drinks that afternoon…but I also saw him here, the night he died," Lana said softly.

"You mean here at the office?" asked Brian.

"Yes," said Lana.

"And you say you had drinks with him? You were at a bar with Peter?" Brian asked.

"Yes," said Lana. "He would take me to the bar across the street for drinks after work once in a while." Her eyes got a dazed look and she shook her head.

"Do you often go out drinking with your colleagues here?" asked Brian.

"No. Only with Peter," Lana said.

"If you don't mind me asking, did you and Peter do anything else outside the office?" asked Brian.

"We occasionally would go out to dinner," said Lana.

"Peter would come around the corner and say 'Hey Lana, it has been a rough day. Let's grab some food' and then he would take me out to dinner."

"What kind of dinner?" asked Brian.

"We usually ate somewhere fancy," said Lana. "Peter would introduce me to other people he knew at fancy clubs around town. I think he liked having me by his side when he went out at night."

"Why is that?" asked Brian.

"Well, sometimes he would call me sweetie…but mostly he loved to brag about what a great secretary I was," said Lana.

"Did you ever go anywhere else with Peter?" asked Brian.

"No. After dinner he would drive me home. He made sure I got safely into my apartment and then he would leave," said Lana. Some new tears were forming in her eyes. She sniffed and pulled out another tissue. "I should really get back to my desk," said Lana.

"Okay," said Brian. "Just one more question, Miss Morris. Do you know Peter's wife Hannah? She mentioned you. Did she call the office often?"

Lana sat up straighter, and her expression darkened. "Yes, actually." She wiped away her tears angrily. "In fact, I am sorry to say this since she just lost her husband, but Hannah Sedgewick is not a nice person. She was always calling and yelling at me if I couldn't put her through to Peter right away. But it wasn't my fault," she exclaimed. "He really was in meetings all the time, or at working lunches. If you ask Mrs. Sedgewick, I bet she thinks I'm a liar. She is a vindictive woman. But I swear to you, Detective. You can ask Mr. Jones if you don't believe me. I would never lie to someone's wife on the phone. This isn't the sixties. We are all professionals here." To Patricia's eyes, the young woman spoke very convincingly, but Lana also kept glancing into the hallway, as if afraid Jeff Jones would reappear.

"Thank you for answering my questions, Lana," said Brian, jotting down a few notes on his notepad.

"You're welcome. If you need anything else, just let me know," said Lana.

"Actually, I was hoping to take a look at Peter's office. Can you let us in?" asked Brian.

"Sure," said Lana. "My keys are at my desk." Patricia and Brian followed Lana back to her desk. Jeff still lingered by the copy machine, which made Patricia uncomfortable. While Lana was sifting through her desk drawer, the elevator opened. A beautiful, professional-looking woman in her forties walked out. She was dressed in a pretty, pale blue linen shift dress with a tailored blazer on top. Patricia guessed she worked elsewhere in the building.

"Hey Lana, I'm here to see Peter. Can I just go back?" the woman asked brightly. Lana's head snapped up. She took a deep breath.

"Oh, Ms. Hendron, haven't you heard?" Lana asked.

"Heard what?" asked Ms. Hendron.

"Peter is dead," said Lana, falling back into her chair with a sob. Ms. Hendron's face fell. She steadied herself on the desk, eyes wide.

"What do you mean he is dead?" the woman asked.

"He died a few days ago," said Lana.

"How—?" the woman started to reply, still in shock.

Lana interrupted her. "Ms. Hendron, this is Detective Johnson. He is investigating what happened to Peter. I'm so sorry you had to find out this way. Would you like to sit down so I can fetch you a drink of water?"

"No, thank you, Lana," Ms. Hendron replied faintly. "I think I will go back to my office downtown."

"Okay," said Lana. "I'm so sorry, Ms. Hendron." Lana looked worried for the older woman. Brian stepped forward and pressed his business card into Susan's hand.

"Please call me if you have any information you think might help the investigation," Brian said to the woman.

She merely looked at his business card in a daze. She seemed to shake herself a little bit but did not reply, and then left.

"How did she know Peter?" asked Brian.

"That was Susan Hendron. She's been friends with Peter since college, I think," said Lana.

"Do you have any way I can get ahold of her?" asked Brian.

"Sure. Just a minute," Lana said. Patricia saw her pull out some keys and a business card. "Here is an extra business card of hers, you can keep it. These are Peter's keys. Do you mind letting yourselves into his office?" Lana asked Brian.

"Sure," said Brian. Lana sniffled into her crumpled tissue again, and Brian and Patricia walked down the hall in the direction she indicated.

Patricia realized Peter's office was the office at the opposite end of the hallway in the corner, just like Jeff's. When they opened the door, they were greeted with the same spectacular view. This time Patricia sighed in admiration and crossed to look out at Atlanta.

"You held that in well when we were in Jeff's office," Brian said with a snort of laughter.

"It hardly seemed appropriate," said Patricia. Something occurred to her and she turned back to face Brian, who was perusing the papers on Peter's desk. "Why didn't you question Susan Hendron?" Patricia asked.

"She just found out about Peter. I am not a monster. I will catch up to her in a few days," said Brian.

"So, where do we begin?" Patricia asked Brian, looking around the office.

"I will search his computer. Why don't you look through his desk drawers?" Brian suggested. Patricia agreed. There were files of old contracts and other business papers. There was nothing pertaining to his personal business, only paperwork related to the company division he managed with Jeff Jones here in downtown Atlanta. She did not find anything that looked helpful for the investigation.

"I am going to have to send someone out to look over this computer," said Brian. "I'm not able to get in." Brian stood up and started looking around the rest of the office.

Patricia finished with the drawers and looked at Peter's desk. There was a picture of his wife and a desk calendar. Patricia opened the calendar and saw a number of dates written in for the past months. Later in the week, he had written down "Aria 8pm" circled in red. Patricia used her phone to take a picture of the note and looked through the calendar some more. There was nothing else interesting there.

"Do you know what I do not see?" asked Patricia.

"What?" Brian asked.

"I do not see anything that would suggest that Peter was into camping. Everything about his home and office suggests a wealthy businessman. The kind who enjoys a good cigar and whisky, fancy dinners. There is nothing to suggest that he liked to go camping," said Patricia. "No pictures of him on top of a mountain or posing in nature."

"That is a good observation," said Brian.

"You already thought of that, didn't you?" Patricia asked. Brian grinned.

"Let's go for now," said Brian. "How about we grab a late lunch?"

"Sure," said Patricia. She followed Brian out. He gave the office key back to Lana and she put it in a drawer. Lana's eyes were red-rimmed, but she seemed to have regained her composure. Patricia followed Brian into the elevator.

"So, what do we do now?" Patricia asked.

"I have a feeling that Lana was not telling us the whole truth," said Brian. "Between Hannah Sedgewick's suspicions and Jeff trying to keep us away from her, I need more information about her." Patricia thought Lana was young and flirty, but not someone who would sleep with her boss. She did not have any evidence of this, just a gut feeling. Brian, however, seemed to think that Lana was simply trying to throw them off the scent with a false sense of morality. They had to rule out whether she was the one Peter was having an affair with.

Brian suggested a nearby deli for lunch. Patricia realized she was very hungry and agreed. They ordered some sandwiches and discussed the case some more. Patricia was stuck on the fact that Peter was found at the campground. Nothing about Peter's life suggested he liked the great outdoors, though something about Lana's tan made Patricia wonder if she spent a lot of time hiking. Brian kept circling Lana as a potential killer if for no other reason than to rule her out.

"What motive did she have?" asked Patricia.

"Maybe he promised her a raise and did not see it through. Or, maybe he told her she could leave the company with him and then changed his mind," Brian said. Patricia admitted that those were good reasons. "Or maybe they really were having an affair and she was jealous." They ate their sandwiches and sipped sweet tea, thinking.

"I'll say one thing…I did not like how Mr. Jones seemed to imply that Lana was mentally unstable. She seemed perfectly normal to me," Patricia said. "Why would Jeff say that about her?"

"I agree that she seemed sad but certainly not unstable. Perhaps he has seen her in other situations that made him think that, however. In any case, I think I will shadow Lana tonight and see where that leads me," Brian said.

"Like a stakeout? Wow. I'd love to see that." Patricia said.

"Would you like to come along?" asked Brian, surprising Patricia. "Two minds are better than one. Why don't I drop you off at your RV and I will pick you up again around six? I saw that Lana has a long meeting scheduled today at five, so she probably will not get out of the office until at least six-thirty. You will want to wear something comfortable. We will be out all night. I will pick up some supplies before I come get you."

"How do you know she has a meeting?" Patricia asked.

"I read her calendar while she was looking for the key," said Brian with a wink.

"Good detecting," said Patricia. They finished their lunch, and Brian drove Patricia back to the campground. She got out of the truck and thought about what she was going to wear that night. Something thrilled her about the idea of spending the night on a stakeout with Brian, even though she told herself it was just business.

# chapter eight

While she was getting ready for the stakeout, Patricia received a text from Tom. He and Valerie were inviting Patricia for dinner. Patricia sent a text back declining the invitation. She felt a twinge of guilt. Tom and Valerie had been so nice to her. She knew Valerie wanted to know the outcome of her conversation with Brian—little did her new friend know how far things had progressed since that day they had gone shopping together. Patricia hoped she would be able to tell them the truth soon.

Patricia donned a comfortable top and her favorite dark jeans. She slipped on a pair of red Converse sneakers and grabbed a jean jacket against the night chill. Suddenly she stopped. She thought about what Lana had told them. She texted Brian and got changed. Patricia put her jeans, sneakers and jacket in her gym bag and put the bag on her bed.

Patricia changed into an evening outfit. She chose a floral dress in a flowing bohemian style that looked nice enough for cocktail attire once she paired it with a fancy bolero shrug and the perfect earrings and necklace. Lana had mentioned that Peter liked to take her to exclusive clubs. If that was the kind of thing she did in her spare time, Patricia and Brian would not be able to follow her inside if they wore jeans and sneakers. Patricia stepped into a pair of heels to match her dress. She put on some more makeup and waited for Brian to pick her up.

While she was waiting, she received a text from Tom asking if she was okay. Patricia replied that she was fine. She just had to do some more research that night. This was not entirely a lie, she reasoned. Patricia was hoping to get into some clubs so she could write about them for her article. She had not planned on writing a lot about Atlanta's nightlife, but since the situation had arisen, she planned to take full advantage of it. She hoped that Tom and Valerie would not ask too many questions. She hated to disappoint her new friends.

Patricia heard Brian's truck drive up. It was his truck, not the police department SUV that he sometimes drove, which would allow them to go unnoticed during the stakeout. She grabbed her gym bag with the change of clothes in it and her clutch purse and walked outside. Brian whistled.

"You clean up well," he said. Patricia laughed.

"You don't look that bad, either," she replied, feeling a flutter in her chest as he stepped out. Brian wore a nice suit in a slim cut that accented his muscular frame.

"Why thank you, ma'am. And may I say, the gym bag really completes your outfit," Brian replied, laughing. Patricia laughed, too. He towered over her with a warm smile and those beautiful eyes staring into hers.

"Well, I am practical if nothing else," Patricia said nervously to break the tension. Brian nodded and grinned.

"Excited?" he asked, carrying the bag for her. She nodded eagerly, and he held open the truck door for her, a perfect gentleman as usual. They drove downtown to Atlanta.

They arrived at the office building right around the time Brian predicted that Lana would be leaving work. Brian pulled into the parking garage and drove around for a bit before he chose a spot to park in. When Patricia asked him about his choice, Brian explained.

"Pretty standard for this kind of stakeout—I looked up the make and model of Lana's car, and her license plate number. She drives that Nissan Altima over there. From this spot she should not notice us, but we will be able to watch her."

"Good thinking," said Patricia. They waited for about twenty minutes, and the time seemed to tick by slowly. A few people came out of the building and went to their cars. Lana was not one of them. Patricia began to worry they had missed her when Brian focused intently on the building's doors.

"There she is," Brian said, pointing. Lana exited alone. She got into the Altima and pulled out of the garage, and Brian followed her at a discreet distance. Patricia admired Brian's driving skills. He nimbly followed the small Nissan as Lana led them on a confusing route through the downtown traffic towards a residential neighborhood. She pulled over by some row houses.

"This must be where she lives," Patricia said. "Maybe I got dressed up for nothing."

"Well, I like that you got dressed up," said Brian. Patricia smiled to herself. Lana walked up the front steps to a house and let herself in. Brian parked across the street and down a little ways. They were able to see through the windows and watch the front door. A light came on from the second floor. Patricia looked through Brian's binoculars and saw it must be Lana's bedroom right before Lana herself pulled the curtains closed. A few minutes later, the light went off.

"Was that the quickest stakeout in history, or what?" Patricia asked Brian. He held up one finger in a waiting gesture. A few minutes later, Lana re-appeared at the front door. She had on a dark red dress that barely came down to mid-thigh and very high heels accentuated her long, tan legs. Patricia's eyes nearly popped at the tight and revealing dress.

"It seems like you will need your dress after all," Brian

commented as Lana walked to her car. She got in and Brian followed her once more. They followed Lana uptown to a district where there were swanky restaurants and bars catering to the night crowd. After Lana parked, Brian did too, then waited and signaled to Patricia when it was safe to get out. A half-block away, Lana disappeared through a fancy door with a small, tasteful sign to one side reading *The Foxtrot Club* in looping gold letters. This was some place special, Patricia realized.

Patricia and Brian followed her a few minutes later. Brian paid their cover charge and led Patricia to a corner booth. There they were able to see the layout of the club, which was luckily quite spacious despite the mingling crowds. There was no chance that Lana would look over and see them watching her unless she walked right up to the booth. There was a bar along the wall next to a decent-sized dance floor. The music playing sounded like updated big-band dance tunes and it complimented the old fashioned but posh decor. There were couples dancing a quick round on the dance floor. A waitress stopped by and they ordered some soft drinks.

"Could you put mine in a fancy glass with a slice of lime?" Patricia asked.

"Certainly," said the waitress.

"Good call," said Brian, sounding impressed.

"Well, if you're in a club, people expect one of us to be drinking," Patricia laughed. Drink in hand, Patricia scanned the club. Despite the dim lighting and the crowded tables, Patricia spotted Lana by the bar. She nudged Brian. He nodded.

Lana was talking to an older gentleman in a tailored business suit. Lana would lean in and put her hand on his arm every so often. Occasionally she would laugh, and he would smile.

"I guess she is looking for her next sugar daddy," said Brian. Patricia did not like this idea but had to admit it looked like Lana was buttering up this gentleman for a night on the town. Just then, Lana and the first man were joined by another older gentleman who leaned in to speak to Lana as well.

"Wow, she caught two at once," said Brian. "This doesn't look good."

"Let me see if I can get closer. I want to hear what they are saying," said Patricia.

"Okay, but be careful," said Brian. Patricia got up with her drink and walked towards the bar. She kept two or three people between herself and Lana. She pretended to be scanning the dance floor for some friends while she listened over the hubbub of voices to catch some of Lana's conversation.

"I really do miss him," Lana was saying to the first gentleman.

"I know," he replied. "We all do."

"Do you know when the memorial service will be?" asked the other gentleman.

"I think she will hold it at the end of next week," said Lana. Her smile turned into a frown. "I've been meaning to ask you something…I just can't get off my mind what Jeff said the other day about—"

"Don't let it upset you, Lana. Jeff is right. Peter would not want that spreading around. Peter wouldn't want you worrying, either. Here, let me get you another drink," said one of the older men. He held up his hand and the bartender dropped what he was doing immediately and went over to the group.

"I will have another whiskey, and get this young lady whatever she wants," said the older gentleman.

"Will do, sir," said the bartender. Patricia noticed someone else trying to get the bartender's attention, but the bartender ignored them. Instead, he poured the whiskey and a gin and tonic for Lana. Only after serving the group did the bartender pay attention to the other customer. *Usually they do that when they know someone is rich,* thought Patricia. Patricia looked back, and Lana had disappeared. Patricia panicked for a moment and then she felt a hand on her back. She turned her head and Brian was there.

"One of the gentleman took Lana on the dance floor, but they're way over on the other side. Would you like to join them?" Brian asked, holding out his hand. Patricia hesitated, looking around. "No one will recognize us in these fancy clothes, I promise," he reassured her.

"Then I would love to," said Patricia. They stepped onto the dance floor together. Brian held Patricia close, and they danced together well. Although her heart fluttered again to feel him so near, Patricia knew the stakeout was more important and that this romantic setting was a coincidence, just like the Ferris wheel had been. Patricia tried to focus and told Brian what she had overheard Lana saying.

Brian frowned. He agreed that it seemed like the gentlemen were trying to console Lana, not romance her. More importantly, what did Jeff not want Lana to spread around? Something that Peter would not have liked to be talked about either, it seemed. Between the questioning and behavior they had witnessed at the office and Lana's words that night, Brian and Patricia agreed that Jeff Jones knew more than he was letting on.

Patricia spied Lana across the dance floor through a break in the crowd and nodded her head in that direction to signal Brian her location. Lana was dancing with her partner, but the older gentleman stood at a respectful distance. He might have been her kindly grandfather, intent on cheering her up with a glamorous twirl on the dance floor. There was no flirting. Brian agreed with her. The song ended, and Brian escorted Patricia back to the table before Lana could see them.

Lana continued to talk to the older men at the bar for another half hour. Then she put down her drink and kissed them both on their cheeks. One of the gentlemen held her hands in his and said something to her. Lana's eyes filled with tears. She hugged him and went to get her coat.

Brian told Patricia he had already paid for their drinks, so they stood to follow Lana out. Patricia stepped into the restroom while Brian watched the club's front door carefully for Lana's exit. As Patricia locked the stall door behind her, she was shocked to hear Lana's voice entering the ladies' room, apparently talking into her mobile phone. "Yes, they were too sweet. You were right. It was a good idea to come here first." There was a zipping sound as Lana opened her purse. Patricia peeked through the tiny gap in the stall door and saw Lana take out a lipstick and reapply it. She hid again, nervous that Lana might catch a glimpse of her somehow.

The younger woman continued her conversation. "Okay, Jeff. I should be there in about fifteen minutes. See you soon… I love you." Then she ended the call and Patricia heard the click of Lana's heels exiting the restroom. She crossed her fingers that Lana had not seen Brian. When she stepped out of the ladies' room, he told her he had been well concealed among the crowd. Lana had left seconds before.

"Brian, she was talking to Jeff," Patricia said urgently, her ears feeling like they were on fire from overhearing the conversation in the restroom. "They've both been lying to us. Lana said 'I love you' to him. I think they're having an affair."

"It seems this night has just begun," said Brian, clenching his jaw. He clutched Patricia's hand and they walked quickly back to the truck to continue following Lana.

After a tense fifteen minutes, Patricia and Brian had followed Lana's car to a different nightclub district. It seemed to cater to a younger, hipper crowd, with live music spilling out from a few venues and themed dance nights advertised on marquees. Lana ducked into a club, much larger and louder than the first one. Brian and Patricia ducked in after her. Patricia wondered if Lana and Jeff had picked this club deliberately. The lights and loud music made it difficult to see or hear much. The club seemed crowded. Patricia worried that they would lose Lana. She looked around for Jeff or Lana but could not see anything.

Brian led Patricia to a stairway that went up to a small lofted area in the corner filled with booths overlooking the dance floor. Finally, they spied Lana by the bar. She was talking to a well-dressed younger man. By the fancy headphones slung around his neck, Patricia guessed the young man must be a DJ. He smiled at Lana, then took her into his arms and kissed her for quite a while. Patricia was as surprised as Brian.

"What happened to meeting up with Jeff Jones?" asked Brian.

"I wonder," Patricia replied, mystified. She decided to go to the bar and find out. Brian said he would keep watch from his vantage point. Patricia navigated through the crowds to the bar, only a few people away from where Lana stood, and got the bartender's attention. She requested cola with lime in a nice glass, telling the bartender she was the designated driver with a big smile. With her virgin drink in hand, Patricia leaned against the bar and tuned into Lana's conversation.

# chapter nine

"It is so good to see you," Lana said to the handsome blond man. He circled his arm around her waist and pulled her in for another kiss.

"I've missed you, darling," he said to Lana. Even over the noise of the club, Patricia could hear that he spoke in an English accent.

"I've been so busy with work," said Lana. "I've been going crazy missing you."

"I understand," he replied. He ran a hand through his stylish haircut as he watched Lana. "I just wish you didn't have to work so hard these days. Your stupid boss works you too hard."

Patricia perked up her ears when she heard this. So the young DJ knew about Jeff Jones. Was there going to be some kind of confrontation? She hoped Brian was ready to step in, if that happened. Yet the young man seemed oddly calm when he mentioned Lana's boss. Patricia was confused.

"He's not stupid. And you know I would spend all my time with you if I could," Lana replied. "Everything has been a mess since Peter's death."

"Let me get you a drink." The young man got the

bartender's eye and ordered two gin and tonics. He handed one to Lana.

"To Peter," he said, raising his glass. Lana seemed to get choked up. The young man lowered his drink and put his arms around Lana. Lana rested her head on his shoulder. She seemed to be crying.

"I have to stop this," said Lana, taking a deep breath after a while.

"It's okay," said the man gently. "I'm here for you, love."

"It just doesn't seem fair," said Lana. "I wait all day to see you and we end up talking about Peter again."

"It's okay, Lana. I know how much he meant to you," the man replied.

"He really did," said Lana. "I don't know where I would be without him."

"He saw in you exactly what I do," came the response. "He knew how good you are at your job, and that you would be even better when he helped you get a new job with bigger responsibilities. He believed in you."

"Yes, he did," Lana responded, wiping her eyes. "I was just talking to Jim and Saul at the other club. Jim wanted to talk to me about something."

"Really? What did he want?"

"Well, he told me I could come and work for him if I wanted to," said Lana.

"That is fantastic, babe. Why didn't you tell me when you got here? This is huge news. You don't have to work for that other Jeff anymore. We should celebrate!" At the excitement in the young man's voice, Lana jumped off her barstool and hugged him. *That other Jeff? What on earth,* wondered Patricia. As Patricia watched, Lana gave him another big kiss.

"I love you so much. Let's go dance before your DJ set starts," Lana said. "Will you let me sit in the booth with you tonight?"

"Only if you answer me one question. Am I your favorite Jeff?" teased the handsome blond, leaning close to her.

"You're the only Jeff that matters," Lana replied with a smile. Holding hands, the young couple swiftly disappeared into the crowd on the dance floor.

Patricia sat on her stool for a moment, digesting everything she had heard. When Brian walked up, he gave her a questioning look.

"Well, that is not what I expected," Patricia said with a laugh. "That's her boyfriend, and his name is Jeff. She was talking to him on the phone earlier, not to her boss." She explained the rest of what she had heard. A look of comprehension came over Brian's features.

"That explains his fancy headphones, too," he said. He leaned over and picked up a little leaflet advertising that night's drink specials. At the top was a name, *DJ Jeff from London,* listing the times he would be playing sets at the club. From the crowd around them, evidently, he was quite popular.

"Unfortunately," Brian said, shaking his head, "this also means Lana is pretty much a dead end in this investigation. She wasn't having an affair with our victim, and she doesn't seem to have any motivation to harm him." He seemed lost in his thoughts. They turned to watch Lana and Jeff across the dance floor, gazing into each other's eyes affectionately. Just then, Jeff looked down at his watch and whispered in Lana's ear, and together they walked over to the DJ booth, far across the vast dance floor from where Patricia and Brian stood.

"I guess we won't be seeing much more of them tonight," Patricia commented.

"Yes," Brian said. "I'm sorry I brought you along on this stakeout and it turned out to be such a bust." He gave her an apologetic look.

"This has been a lot of fun, though," said Patricia. The nightclub pulsed around them with music and conversation.

With a sinking feeling in her stomach, she wondered if this was the end of their evening together. Perhaps Brian felt the same way, because he kept giving her sideways looks as they watched the dancers. They were both reluctant to break the spell.

# chapter ten

Brian ran a hand through his wavy brown hair, which had tumbled down over his forehead a little bit in the warmth of the club. He looked at Patricia. "What are you thinking?" he asked quietly.

Questions swirled in Patricia's mind. She wanted to spend more time with Brian, but she tried to keep her mind on the investigation. After all, that was the purpose of this evening. "I was thinking that the stakeout isn't a total bust. We can still question Jeff Jones about what Lana said, right?"

Brian chuckled, as if surprised by her answer. "Absolutely. But that can wait until tomorrow. Right now, the stakeout is over."

"Okay," said Patricia, hiding her disappointment. "I can catch a taxi from here, you don't have to drive me all the way back to the campground."

"I didn't say it was time to go home," Brian protested. He smiled at her warmly. "Maybe I want you to stay for a little while."

"Really?" said Patricia, a slow blush warming her cheeks. The flutter in her chest returned whenever Brian smiled at her like that. She liked it a lot and only wanted it to continue. She was glad he wanted to spend more time with her, too.

"Besides, it would be a shame to waste that pretty dress," he said. Brian took her hand and guided her out of the club. He saw a cab and hailed it.

"What about your truck?" Patricia asked.

"It is fine in the lot," said Brian. "This way we won't have to walk back." Patricia grinned, wondering what he was planning. Brian held the cab door open and Patricia jumped in. Brian gave the taxi an address and they sped across town.

The cab stopped at an old warehouse. Patricia looked at Brian skeptically.

"What is this place?" she asked.

"You'll see," said Brian. He paid the taxi driver and helped Patricia out of the car. Patricia noticed a few people outside one of the warehouse doors. She followed Brian to the entrance. The building was old and had some interesting architectural features outside. Looking more closely, Patricia realized it was not a warehouse, but an old train terminal. Through the doorway she glimpsed glittering lights and a beautifully restored interior. *You can't judge a book by its cover,* Patricia thought to herself once again.

"Let's go in," Brian said. He cradled her hand in the crook of his elbow and escorted her inside. They strolled through a large hall with soaring rafters. At the far end there was a small restaurant. Twinkling lights led out onto a terrace for outdoor eating, and the soft breezes wafted through the restaurant. Patricia and Brian sat at a table and a waiter approached.

"Good evening, welcome to The Depot. Can I bring you something to drink?" he asked Patricia and Brian.

"We will have the drink special," said Brian.

"What is the drink special?" asked Patricia after the waiter left.

"Every night they feature a different local craft beer," said Brian. "I think you'll like the one they have on tap tonight. It's an IPA flavored with Georgia peach and aged in whiskey barrels, made right here in Atlanta."

"That sounds delicious," said Patricia.

"I thought you might like that. As for myself, I am off-duty for the night and want to celebrate the newest investigator on my team." He grinned at her, and she felt happy they were working together so well.

The waiter came back with their drinks and listed the nightly specials. Everything was fresh and organic. Patricia chose a delicious salad with citrus crusted shrimp. She was so happy just to be sitting there with Brian. They talked and laughed about so many things while they ate that she lost track of time. Patricia was surprised to see how late the hour was when they finished up dinner and Brian paid the check. Her thoughts turned back to the stakeout that had kicked off their evening together.

"So, what comes next for the investigation?" Patricia asked.

"Well, Peter might not have been having an affair. But maybe Hannah didn't know that," said Brian.

"She really did not like Lana," said Patricia. "Still, even without an affair, there could still be an issue of jealousy."

"What do you mean?" asked Brian.

"He was helping Lana get ahead in the business. Jeff said he was a nice guy who always helped others. Lana said he was helping her to find a better job—he introduced her to those gentlemen at the first club, and one of them did offer her a job today. Hannah could have been jealous that Peter was spending so much time with Lana," said Patricia.

"Jealousy can be a motive for murder. I've seen that before," said Brian.

"Are you going to question Hannah again?" asked Patricia.

"Yes. But first, I need to check out the banking angle, and the autopsy report should come back soon about whether there were any illegal substances in Peter's body at the time of death. Despite Hannah claiming there were no financial problems, Jeff Jones made me wonder if this latest club deal was in financial difficulty and he was hiding it from his wife. I'll need to get a warrant to access his financial records with Imperial Capital and examine the matter closely," Brian said.

"I understand. Let me know what you find out from the autopsy report," she said. "What about following up with Jeff Jones?"

"That, too. But it might be better if I go back to question him alone," he said. Patricia nodded. She was glad he had allowed her to help this much so far.

When they were done with dinner, Brian told Patricia to follow him. They went through a large archway into an outdoor stage area surrounded by a small garden. A local band was just starting to play. Their music was loud and fun. Patricia smiled.

"I think I have heard this song before," she said to Brian.

"Probably in my truck, I love this album. They also had a few hits on the radio a while back," Brian replied. They listened to the music and danced. It was late, and the starry skies above grew chilly, but as they danced, Patricia felt all of her worries melting away. Music was the ultimate release. After the band was done, Patricia and Brian decided to walk back to his truck instead of taking a taxi.

"I know a late-night coffee shop a little ways from here. Want to walk there for a nightcap?" asked Brian. Patricia said yes. She did not want the night to end.

They walked together down the quiet city streets. Brian told her stories about going to concerts during his college years and it made her laugh so hard her cheeks ached from smiling. They talked about different bands and kinds of music they enjoyed.

At the coffee shop door, Brian held her arm as they

walked in. Her feet were aching after the long night. "Coffee sounds good right about now," she said.

"Here, have a seat," said Brian, pulling a chair out from a table by the front window. "I will go and get some coffee for us."

"Thank you," said Patricia. It felt good to sit down. Brian came back a moment later with two steaming cups of coffee.

"What a wild night," said Patricia. Brian laughed.

"I like your definition of wild night," he said. Patricia joined in his laughter.

"I suppose this is tame compared to some nights you must have had on the job," said Patricia.

"You've got that right," said Brian. They sipped their coffee and Patricia looked out the window. The city lights gleamed everywhere around them. Being in the middle of Atlanta at night was exciting. At least she was with a police officer to keep her safe.

"I love a city at night," Patricia said.

"So do I," said Brian. "There's a different vibe at night." He looked at her with a warm smile again and she wondered if he was still talking about the city.

"Yes. It's something hard to describe," Patricia agreed. They finished their coffees in companionable quiet, neither wanting to break the moment. When Brian finally used his phone to call them an Uber back to his truck, Patricia sighed. It was bittersweet. When they got to his truck, he came around to open the door and help Patricia out of the taxi.

"I had a great evening," said Patricia.

"I'm glad," said Brian. "Should I drop you at your RV?"

"Actually, I think I'm going to take this Uber, if you don't mind." She signaled the driver, who nodded and waited. "Tom and Valerie are starting to get suspicious of me. I don't want them to know I am involved with…this investigation," said Patricia. *Or am I worried they will think I am involved with this handsome detective?* The thought made the butterflies in her stomach flutter again.

"That's smart," said Brian. "I don't want them to get too involved." He seemed to be lingering, waiting for her to say the last word. Finally, she could delay no longer. She gave him a quick hug.

"Goodnight, Brian. Thanks for a beautiful night." She stood at the open door of the taxi.

"My pleasure," he said. He stood at the door to his truck and waited for her to climb in the taxi, then waved goodbye.

Patricia changed into her sneakers in the back of the Uber and felt like the luckiest woman alive. Even without a goodnight kiss, it had been one of the best dates ever.

# chapter eleven

Patricia had the driver drop her off at the entrance to the Stone Mountain campground, wanting to walk through the quiet night by herself for a while. She strolled in the moonlight to her RV and thought back to everything that had happened that night. Her feet felt better in her sneakers. It was well after midnight and the campground was quiet, only crickets and frogs to keep her company. Patricia did not want to have to lie to Tom and Valerie again about why she was out so late in such fancy clothes. She crossed her fingers, hoping they had gone to bed already. To hedge her bets, she took the long way around the campground and walked toward the mountain. She had not seen it this late at night.

When Patricia got to the tree line, she stopped and pulled her flashlight out. She followed the beam to the edge of the woods. There in front of her stood the mountain. It was tall and ominous at night. Patricia was in awe of the size of the carving on the side of the mountain. The full moon accentuated the cuts in the rock of the mountain. Patricia heard a noise and turned around. There was an armadillo crossing the path behind her and waddling towards the forest. Patricia giggled, telling herself not to be so easily scared.

She walked a bit along the trail at the base of the mountain. The evening had been too much of an adrenaline rush for her to go right back to her RV. Patricia met a park ranger patrolling in a golf cart.

"Can I help you, ma'am?" asked the park ranger.

"No, thank you," said Patricia. "I am just enjoying the beautiful evening."

"Okay. Be careful where you walk," the park ranger said. "I think we have some snakes out early this year." Patricia shivered. She had not thought about snakes coming out at night.

"I will, sir. Thank you," Patricia said. The ranger drove on and Patricia circled back towards her RV. All in all, her trip to Atlanta had been a whirlwind—not just the research for her article, but also the investigation with Brian. She remembered with a shock that she had not replied to Lenore about the Paris trip yet. Patricia needed to give her editor an answer soon.

She rounded the corner and heard a noise by her RV. Patricia shone her light on the ground by the RV and saw something move. She held her breath and stopped short. A few seconds later, an opossum sauntered by Patricia. Three tiny baby opossums gripped onto the fur of its back. The mother opossum hissed at her and then went on its way. Patricia smiled. Some people did not like the creatures, but she thought opossums were cute.

Patricia turned off her flashlight. The hush of the forest seemed to be growing a little breezy and the air smelled like rain. In the sky, she could see the moonlight reflecting off of an approaching bank of thunderclouds. Fatigue seemed to finally get the best of her and she was ready to turn in for the night, especially if a rain storm was on its way.

By the time she was fumbling around her purse for her

key, the moon had disappeared behind the clouds. The rain was definitely coming. She walked up to the RV door and unlocked it, happy to be home.

Then, as she opened the door, she felt something hit the back of her head. Hard. Patricia cried out and fell. Darkness closed in.

When Patricia awoke, her head throbbed. The pain was almost unbearable, and she was terribly cold. She moved slightly, and pain seared though her scalp. Patricia realized she was soaking wet and lying on the steps, halfway into her RV. Around her, the rain pelted down, turning the campground into a sodden, muddy mess. She turned her head and looked behind her. Her heart pounded in her throat and she wondered if her assailant was simply waiting to make another move. Patricia listened for a moment and did not hear anything over the pouring rain. She thought about trying to move and the pounding in her head made it seem impossible. She waited, hoping the pain would subside. It did not.

Lightning flashed and thunder struck somewhere nearby, and the loud sound made her head ache even worse. She was shivering from the rain, and every shiver made the pain in her skull worse, too. Patricia made up her mind. She had to get inside. She put her hands on the floor and pushed. Her head did not like that at all. She then tried to roll over. She got about halfway and had to stop. She could not tell if the flashes in front of her eyes were from the lightning or if the pain itself was blinding her.

In one last desperate effort, Patricia took a deep breath and forced herself to rise up onto her elbows. The sudden nausea was too much. Blinding pain overtook her in a wave. Patricia blacked out.

# chapter twelve

When Patricia came to again, she felt trapped, hands holding her arms down. She tried to wriggle free, but a voice protested and held her tighter.

"Patricia, keep still. It's me, Tom," said a male voice. He sounded far away. Patricia stopped struggling. She slowly opened her eyes and focused on a face nearby. Patricia recognized Tom.

"I think she is coming to," she heard Tom calling out to someone else. "Patricia, can you hear me?" Patricia nodded but then stopped. It hurt too much.

"Okay, Patricia. You are in your RV. Valerie and I heard you yell and when we got here you were unconscious," Tom explained. "Do you know what happened?" Patricia tried to shake her head, but the pain stopped her again and she gasped instead.

"Nevermind," said Tom. "Don't try to speak, okay? The ambulance will be here in a moment."

*Brian,* thought Patricia, *Brian is coming and he will know what to do.* She was shivering with cold and her head felt like it had been hit by a sledgehammer, but she knew Brian would keep her safe. Relieved, she closed her eyes. Tom shook her gently.

"I am sorry, Patricia, but the 911 operator said we have to keep you awake. You don't have to move or talk, but can you keep your eyes open?" Tom asked. "We are afraid you might have a concussion."

Patricia did not want to keep her eyes open. She wanted to go to sleep. Sleep was where she felt warm and safe. She wanted to dream about dancing with Brian. Brian who would be here any minute. Every time she closed her eyes, though, Tom nudged her awake. Why wouldn't he let her sleep? She just wanted to get warm.

In the far distance, Patricia heard a siren wailing. It was quickly drawing closer.

"They're coming," said Tom. He sounded worried. Patricia wanted to reassure him that she was fine. She just needed to rest. Patricia hurt all over, but her head felt the worst. She gathered her strength and tried to ask Tom if he had seen anyone when he came over. Her words came out garbled.

"Did I see anyone?" Tom asked. "No. Why? Was there someone else here with you before? Was it that detective guy, Brian?" Tom's face clouded over with suspicion. Patricia tried to explain to Tom, but she felt too woozy and the warmth of sleep was calling her.

"Valerie," Tom called. "Patricia says someone else was here. She must have been hit on the head. She did not fall."

Patricia saw a look of fear flash across Valerie's face. She and Tom exchanged worried looks. Patricia wanted to reassure Valerie, but she could not move without pain shooting through her head.

"Stay with me, Patricia. Keep your eyes open, okay? Listen. We thought you fell and hit your head," said Tom. "When we got here you were by yourself. The way you were sprawled on the stairs, it looked like you might have fallen. When I saw all the blood, I told Valerie to call 911. They are on the way. Just hold on for a little while longer." Patricia sighed. She was glad that Tom and Valerie were there to help her, but she wanted Brian. She felt terribly dizzy trying to focus on Tom's face. Every time she tried to recall what had happened, the nausea took over.

Was it seconds or minutes later when the ambulance finally arrived? All Patricia knew was that the paramedics took over. They took Patricia's blood pressure and examined her head. Patricia saw a light flashing in her eyes. She heard someone talking, but they were talking too low for Patricia to make out what they were saying. The paramedics wrapped Patricia in a deliciously warm blanket and put a collar on her neck to stabilize her head and then lifted her onto a gurney. Patricia moaned. The paramedic placed an IV into her arm before they moved her further. Her mouth felt like it was filled with cotton. Tom asked which hospital they were taking her to. They gave him the hospital name and address, and Tom said he and Valerie would follow the ambulance. A familiar-looking police SUV arrived as Patricia was being loaded into the ambulance.

From her gurney, she strained to watch the vehicle through the open doors of the ambulance. Then a portly officer with a bushy mustache climbed out and began collecting evidence from her RV steps.

No Brian in sight.

The ambulance doors closed. "I am going to give you some pain medicine," said a voice. "You might start to feel sleepy. You can rest now, it's okay." Cold liquid in the IV rushed into her veins and dimmed the pain. Soon Patricia was sleeping and dreaming of falling.

Patricia woke up. She lay still in clean white sheets. The pain that throbbed inside her head had quieted to a dull roar, though her whole body ached. At least the shivers had finally abated. She realized she was wearing a hospital gown and her beautiful dress was gone. She hoped fleetingly that it had not been ruined.

"Patricia, are you awake? It's me, Valerie," said a voice. Patricia turned her head carefully to avoid making it hurt. Valerie was sitting beside her. She looked worried.

"Where am I?" Patricia asked.

"You are in North County Memorial Hospital," said Valerie. Her voice was soft and gentle. Just then, another voice spoke up from across the room, and Patricia saw Tom standing at the foot of her bed. Tension filled his usually calm form.

"Do you remember what happened last night?" he asked.

"I remember pulling out my key and opening my door. Something hit me on the head and I guess I blacked out," said Patricia.

"That's right," said Tom. "Do you know who did this to you?"

"No," said Patricia. She tried to lift her head, but she felt dizzy. She rested her head back on the pillow.

"Well, the police want to talk to you. I am sure the doctor wants to check you out again this morning, too," said Tom. He glanced at Valerie and she nodded and stepped out to alert the medical staff that Patricia was awake.

"This morning? How long have I been here?" Patricia asked, confused. "Is Brian here?" asked Patricia.

"Do you mean Detective Johnson? No, he isn't," said Tom with an angry look. "Why do you ask?"

"No reason," said Patricia. *Why is Tom so angry about this?*

"You got here last night. Valerie and I stayed the night with you. We've been worried sick. Are you sure you don't remember seeing a man, just before you fell?" Tom asked, stepping closer to her bedside. "You don't remember anything?"

"Yes…no. I mean, I don't remember. Please," said Patricia, "can I have a drink of water?" She was indeed thirsty, but she was also desperate to put some space between her and Tom. His intensity was confusing. Was it mere worry, or was it something else? She did not feel the nausea she had felt the night before. Now she just felt a dull throb in her head. There was also a bandage on her forehead, just under the hairline.

*Someone must have been waiting for me last night,* Patricia thought. *Someone who knew I was staying at the campground.* Tom seemed awfully certain it was a man. Why? The question sent a chill down her spine. She really wanted to talk to Brian, but she did not see her cell phone anywhere.

Her door opened, and a man in a white coat came in.

"Hello, Patricia, I am Dr. Murray," said the doctor. "How are you feeling today?"

"Like someone hit my head with a two-by-four," Patricia answered. She closed her eyes in pain. When she opened them, she saw Tom leaving the room and she breathed a sigh of relief.

"Well, you have a mild concussion. We also had to stitch up that little headwound you got when you fell." He moved her hair aside to check the stitches. "I want you to stay here for observation. If you are feeling better by the afternoon, I will consider releasing you," said the doctor. "Any questions?"

"Why are my wrists sore?" asked Patricia, flexing them carefully.

"You probably held them out instinctually to catch yourself as you were falling. You are lucky they did not break. You have a mild sprain on both sides, but some pain medication will help with that," Dr. Murray replied. "It doesn't require a brace, just be careful with it. No lifting heavy weights for a couple weeks."

"Thank you, Dr. Murray," said Patricia.

"There is a police officer outside who would like to ask you some questions," said the doctor. "Do you feel up to speaking with him?"

"Yes," said Patricia eagerly, nodding at Dr. Murray. *Finally*, she thought, *Brian had arrived.* Anyone transported by a 911 call was listed by name in the police logs that were read by everyone in the precinct, especially if foul play was suspected.

"As long as you are feeling up to it," Dr. Murray said. "If you start to feel dizzy or tired, please stop and get some rest."

"I will," promised Patricia. Dr. Murray left, and a young police officer walked in.

"Hello, Patricia, I am Officer Smith," the man said.

"Hello," said Patricia. She tried to swallow her disappointment that it wasn't Brian.

"Can you tell me what you remember about last night?" Officer Smith asked Patricia. He offered her a sympathetic smile. He seemed to think the look on her face was due to painful memories.

Patricia recounted the same vague details she had given everyone else. It was no help to the police and no help to her, either. They had not found anyone suspicious in the campground and there were no leads yet. Officer Smith promised to get back in touch with her soon, but she did not hold out much hope.

Valerie reappeared and stepped over to Patricia's side when the officer left.

"How are you feeling? Can I get you anything?" Valerie asked Patricia.

"No, thank you. My head is throbbing, and I am still a little dizzy, but at least I'm not nauseous anymore," said

Patricia. She hesitated, wanting to ask for her cell phone so she could call Brian. Something stopped her, however. If he had seen her name in the police log and not come to the scene and also not come to the hospital, perhaps she was crazy to think he would want to. They had shared a special night, but that did not mean he was obliged to help her out on her sickbed. Besides, the doctor said it was just a mild concussion—maybe she shouldn't bother him with something so minor.

She offered a weak smile to Valerie. "I'm just ready to go home."

"I'm glad you're feeling a little better," said Valerie. "Now, we'll be in the waiting room until the doctor discharges you. Ring the bell for the nurse if you want them to fetch us, okay?"

"Okay," Patricia said. The young couple exited her room. In the quiet they left behind, fatigue washed over her. She closed her eyes and a few minutes later, she drifted off.

When she next awoke, Patricia felt a little less groggy. Afternoon light shone outside, and the clock read two. This time the pain in her head and elsewhere was extremely diminished. Patricia was actually able to lift her head off the pillow. She rang for a nurse and after a few minutes, a young nurse appeared in her doorway.

"I would like to try and get dressed. Are my clothes here?" Patricia asked the nurse.

"Yes," the nurse responded. She came over to Patricia's bedside and helped her to stand. "Your things are in the closet—this is everything the paramedics said you had with you." She left Patricia to her privacy and said she would notify the doctor she was nearly ready to be discharged.

Patricia thanked her and looked in the closet. Her dress

from the night before was dry but wrinkled. Patricia felt foolish putting the dress back on, but she wanted to get out of the hospital. She saw her purse and checked inside. No cell phone.

*I wonder if it fell out when I got hit,* Patricia thought as she got dressed. Soon after, her doctor reappeared.

"It looks like you are ready for a night on the town," Dr. Murray joked.

"A night in my own bed will suit me just fine," said Patricia. "So, can I leave?"

"I will discharge you as long as you promise to follow up if you have any severe headaches. If you are vomiting, come right back to the emergency room," Dr. Murray directed.

"I will," said Patricia.

It only took a few minutes to sign her discharge papers and get her pain prescription. The nurse wheeled her out to the front door in a wheelchair. She protested, but the nurse insisted that it was mandatory for her safety.

Tom and Valerie drove up to the curb. "Are you ready to spring this joint?" Valerie asked with a grin.

"I sure am," said Patricia. She hopped in and they were quickly headed back towards the campground.

"Do you want to grab something to eat, or would you like to go right back to the campground?" asked Tom.

"As much as I would like to eat, I think I should get back to my RV," said Patricia.

"Okay," said Tom, giving her a cautious look in the rearview mirror. They drove Patricia back to the campground.

"Why don't you park by your RV, Tom? I think I may have dropped my phone last night and I don't want you to accidently run over it," said Patricia.

"Are you sure you can walk that far?" asked Tom.

"I'll be fine," said Patricia.

"We will walk with you," insisted Valerie. "That way we can help you look for your phone."

"Thank you," said Patricia. "I appreciate that." They pulled into Tom and Valerie's parking area and everyone got out of the car. Patricia walked slowly to her RV, keeping an eye on the walking path and the green shrubs to either side. Valerie walked by her side and Tom followed them. As they rounded the corner to the RV, Patricia saw her phone. Just as she was reaching down to pick up the phone, she heard Valerie gasp. Patricia looked back at Valerie. Valerie had one hand to her mouth and the other was pointing at Patricia's RV. Patricia looked up and almost choked.

On the outside of her RV someone had painted *GO BACK WHERE YOU CAME FROM* in dripping, bright red spray paint. Patricia felt woozy and Tom ran over to steady her. He led Patricia to her picnic table. Patricia sat down. She put her head in her hands and felt all of the emotion from the past couple days spill over. Patricia started to cry. Valerie came over and sat beside her. She put her arm around Patricia and held her tight.

Meanwhile, Tom was on his mobile phone calling the ranger station. Through her tears, Patricia vaguely heard his angry words as he demanded an answer about how someone could have done this in a state park.

Finally, Patricia took a deep breath and wiped her eyes. "Okay," she said. "I got that out of my system." She blew her nose.

"Why would someone do this?" Valerie asked. "First you get assaulted in the middle of the night, and now this…what on earth does it mean? Who could possibly wish you harm?"

Tom finished his phone call with the ranger and came over. "Patricia, I have to level with you. I don't think you're being honest with us." He looked at her sternly. Guilt clutched at her heart. "This Detective Johnson fellow has given us no answers about whether we're safe here even though a murder took place just a few nights ago, and now this second violent incident. What if it was the murderer?

What if the person who killed that other guy tried to kill you, too? Detective Johnson seems to like you and I know you've seen him a bit…is there something he's told you? Something we don't know?"

Patricia decided it was time to confess. "I have been working with Brian on the case."

"I knew it," said Valerie, perking up. "Tom thought he was hitting on you, but I said you were helping him."

"Well…you're both correct. He did take me out on a date after a stakeout last. I didn't want to tell you because you two seemed so worried about me getting involved in the investigation. I was just so excited to finally get back to detective work…"

Valerie reassured her that they were not angry and only wanted to ensure her safety.

Patricia was relieved. She wanted to reassure them, too. "I trust Brian when he says we are not in any danger from a killer roaming Stone Mountain campground. What happened to me was probably just a coincidence," Patricia said. Her head was starting to pound again.

Tom did not look convinced by her words. "We should call him and discuss this, in any case. There's too many similarities between the two incidents. Where is your phone? You don't look in any shape to make a phone call." Patricia handed over her phone. Tom called Brian's cell phone but there was no answer.

"He must be busy with the case," Tom said. Instead, he texted him and told him what had happened to Patricia's RV and said she was back from the hospital. He gave the phone back to Patricia.

"I am sure he will call or stop by as soon as he can," said Valerie hopefully. Patricia looked at her poor vandalized trailer and sighed. Tom said that the ranger was waiting for Officer Smith who had taken her statement at the hospital, and they would come photograph her RV for evidence.

"I will wait with you until they get here," said Valerie.

"Thank you," Patricia said. She was still in shock. A little while later, Officer Smith arrived with the park ranger and took some photographs of the RV and looked around. He did not find anything.

"You haven't remembered anything else about what happened, have you?" he asked Patricia.

"No," she sighed. Patricia's headache was back. She guessed the pain medication from the hospital was probably wearing off and it was time to take her prescription soon. "Who do you think did this to my vehicle?"

"Hard to say, ma'am. It could be the same person who assaulted you, it could be someone else. You did say that only a few people know you are here in town. Have you come into contact with many locals?" he asked.

"Not many who know that I'm staying here, no." She did not want to reveal to him that she was helping with the questioning for the murder investigation. Patricia was not sure how much Officer Smith knew about her involvement and she did not want to get Brian in trouble, just in case.

"Well, it could also simply be a case of bad blood between neighbors," the officer offered.

"What do you mean?" she asked, shocked. Valerie and Tom looked concerned as well.

"With the murder investigation and then you getting picked up by the ambulance…could be someone in the park blames you." He gave her an apologetic look. "I'm not saying I believe that, no decent person would. But you never know when folks on vacation will see a few things and jump to the wrong conclusions, you know?"

Patricia nodded, stunned at this possibility. She was suddenly overcome by fatigue and could not wait to lie down to sleep. "Thank you for your help," Patricia said. After the officer left, Patricia told Tom and Valerie to go back to their place.

"I need to rest," Patricia explained. "I appreciate everything you've done for me." Valerie gave Patricia a hug.

"We will be back to check on you later," said Tom.

"Don't worry about me," said Patricia. "I will probably just sleep until tomorrow." It was late afternoon at this point, and she guessed an early bedtime would do her good.

"If you need us, just call," said Tom. Tom and Valerie waved goodbye and walked back to their RV.

Patricia looked at her phone once more and sighed. There was still no message back from Brian. Tears threatened again, so Patricia went into her RV. She ate a sandwich and took her pain medication, then laid down. She tossed and turned for a while and then got back up. Sleepiness just would not come. She had napped too long at the hospital. Patricia took a long, hot shower and then tried to sit and read. Her mind kept going back to the night before. She thought perhaps it was time for her to move on from Atlanta. Whether it had been a random stranger or someone who knew she was here, both the violent assault and the spray paint incident made her feel the campground was no longer safe. She checked the locks on her RV door again.

Then she remembered that she could not leave the park. With the message spray-painted on its side, Patricia could not drive her RV anywhere. She would have to get some paint remover at the hardware store. Patricia felt worse and worse. She tried Brian again, but there was no answer.

Finally, Patricia made a cup of coffee. There was no use falling into a pit of despair when there was work to do, she told herself. She walked to the bus terminal. She felt a little sorry for herself when her head ached and tried to take it slow. The past two days were swirling around in her mind and Patricia just wanted to escape.

For one thing, she was convinced that her part in the investigation was done. That must be why Brian was not calling back. She remembered him saying last night that he needed to do the next interviews by himself. It was one thing for Patricia to help with the early, easy questions, but now the investigation was getting real. It was not her place to push herself on him if he did not want her assistance.

When the city bus came, she climbed on and watched the scenery out the window on the way to the hardware store. Patricia decided she would clean off the spray paint early the next day, after a good night's sleep. Maybe by then Brian will have gotten back in touch.

As she walked from the bus stop to the hardware store, her phone rang in her pocket, and her heart leapt. But it was not Brian after all.

"Patricia, it's Lenore. How's Atlanta? You must be almost done with your research by now. Are you having fun?" asked Lenore, her chirpy voice reminding Patricia suddenly of the looming deadline for her article. She was disappointed.

"Hi, Lenore. Yes, and I'm almost done writing the article."

"Fantastic. Did you make a decision about Paris?"

Patricia's head felt very confused. The murder investigation swam in her mind along with her feelings for Brian and the dizziness from her pounding headache that had suddenly returned. She took a deep breath.

"Yes. I'll go to Paris."

Lenore whooped with celebratory laughter and started giving her all the details. Patricia listened as best she could and then asked her to send everything by email so she could read it in the morning when her head was clear.

"Everything okay, Patricia? You sound so tired."

"It's just been a long couple of days," she said. She was determined not to tell her editor about the investigation since it was on her own time. She did not want to jeopardize her chance at Paris. They hung up, and Patricia wandered the aisles of the hardware store for a little while, feeling lost.

By the time she paid for the can of paint remover and headed for the bus stop, she was determined to make her last night in Atlanta count. Surely she had earned it, after the last couple of days she had been through.

Patricia headed back to the campground, her fatigue and headache forgotten. She changed into a pretty top and her favorite nice jeans and called a cab to take her to a bar.

# chapter thirteen

Patricia was not one to sit and drink, but she felt the need to think hard about her life. The fact that she was disappointed when Lenore had called upset her. Patricia always looked forward to hearing from her publisher. Usually she lived for deadlines and travel and exciting new opportunities. *What is happening to me?* Patricia thought as she drank her beer. *Why am I feeling torn about going to Paris? This is my dream.* Patricia realized she had been putting Brian ahead of her work. That concerned her. She wanted to help Brian solve his case, but she did not want to risk her career in doing so. The spray paint on her RV was a clear sign that her career needed more attention. It was time to move on. She finished the beer and left the bar.

Patricia wanted to just go somewhere and let go of everything. She had dressed to impress so she decided to go to a club. There was a hip club down the street from the bar, so she walked there. On the way, she could feel her wrists aching again, and was glad she had brought along her prescription in her purse. When she took the pill, she checked her phone. No messages. She scrolled down to Brian's number, but decided against it. She was having too much fun.

When she got to the club, there was good music playing

and a large bar. Patricia ordered a mixed drink. She drank that and then went onto the dance floor. She danced around and enjoyed herself. The tension finally seemed to release from her shoulders. This felt true to her gypsy soul, she realized—the girl who loved to dance and be free.

Patricia went back to the bar and got a beer. She was feeling fine and she wanted to keep going. She danced and escaped in the music awhile longer. A few guys hit on her, but Patricia told them she was just dancing. They backed off and let her dance. Later, she sat down. Her head was starting to feel a bit sore. The stitches hidden under her hair were fine, so Patricia figured it was from the loud music. She went outside to get some fresh air. She was feeling the alcohol, but she was not ready to go back to her RV. Every time she thought of her RV she got depressed. She had a sudden thought. If this was her last night here, she wanted to visit one more special place. Patricia hailed a cab and told the driver to take her "to that skull place in Little Five Points." She fumbled her purse a little as she checked her phone again and sat down in the backseat.

"Are you sure you are okay, miss?" the driver asked.

"What, are you my dad?" Patricia shot back, dropping her bag into her lap. She tried to smile and make it a joke. The driver held up his hands in surrender. He drove quickly through the Atlanta traffic. Patricia knew she should not have anything else to drink. Despite that, she wanted to keep going. Her inner turmoil was silenced by the beautiful night and the crowds of happy people everywhere on the sidewalk.

The cab dropped her off at the front of the Vortex Bar in Little Five Points. Patricia paid the driver and gave him a good tip. Patricia went right into the bar and sat down. It was crowded, and music played. She could hardly believe her first visit was only a couple days ago. It seemed like a lifetime. Patricia felt her buzz fading a bit and gave into the temptation to order a gin and tonic. A good-looking man was sitting beside her. He raised his glass towards her in a toast. When she smiled back at him, he turned to talk to her.

"Hello," said the man, smiling.

"Hi. What's your name?" asked Patricia.

"I'm Paul, how about you?" the man asked. He had a cheesy grin, but Patricia did not mind.

"My name is Patricia," she said. She heard that she slurred her name a bit and giggled.

"Well, Patricia, may I buy your next drink?" Paul asked.

"Yes," said Patricia emphatically. It was nice to be wanted, Patricia thought as she sipped her drink. She finished it quickly as they chatted. Paul asked what she was doing in town.

"I'm a writer. Well, I'm a traveler now. I'm a writer who does not have a home," Patricia giggled. "My home is…I'm a travel writer." She realized she was more tipsy than she thought. Paul smiled when he ordered Patricia another drink.

"Thank you," said Patricia, putting her hand on Paul's thigh when she leaned over to take the glass.

"You're welcome, beautiful," said Paul with a smirk. Patricia smiled and took another sip. She ignored the dizzy feeling. This was her last night in Atlanta, her last fling with this beautiful city. Patricia deserved to be happy.

Patricia and Paul talked some more. At one point, Patricia got up to go to the ladies' room and stumbled. Paul caught her in his arms.

"My hero," said Patricia with a flirtatious smile. By the time she returned from the restroom, Paul had ordered her a beer.

"Why don't you drink that and then we can go back to my place?" Paul suggested.

"Go back to your place? That's nice. Did I tell you I don't have a home to go back to?" said Patricia.

"Yes, you did. Don't worry, darling. Drink up. I will keep you nice and warm tonight," said Paul. He rested his hand on the top of Patricia's thigh. She smiled. A night with a complete stranger seemed like the best idea of all.

She picked up the beer. "You're fun," she said to him with a grin. Paul crowded into her space, moving to stand between Patricia's legs. He whispered in her ear.

"Yeah, I can tell you like to have fun. Do you want to have some freaky fun tonight?" Paul asked. Patricia laughed and put her beer down.

"Come on baby, drink up," Paul insisted. He tried to kiss Patricia, but she ducked her head. Something felt wrong. "What's wrong, baby? Don't you want to feel good?" Paul asked. He nodded at the drink on the bar. "I ordered that especially for you. It's my favorite. It's sweet, just like you…"

"I think I have had enough to drink," Patricia said. The music seemed to press into her skull. She was starting to feel queasy and unsure.

"Hey baby, don't stop now," Paul insisted. "We were just about to get to the good part." He leaned in closer to reach her lips.

Just then, Paul stumbled back as if shoved. "The lady said she has had enough," Patricia heard someone say. Paul frowned.

"Who are you to decide what the lady wants or needs?" Paul said with a flirtatious smirk and tried to step closer to her again. Then Brian appeared over Paul's shoulder and pulled him backward almost violently. Brian's eyes were a little wild when he saw her. He manhandled Paul over to the side and away from Patricia.

"Brian!" she said and jumped up off the barstool. *What is he doing here?* She felt dizzy and embarrassed.

"Do you know this guy?" Paul asked.

"Yes, I do," said Patricia. "This is my friend, Brian."

"I think you should leave now," the detective said to Paul. He took his badge out of his jacket and flashed it at the man.

"Unless you want me to test that drink you were about to give her."

"Test it for what?" Paul said belligerently. "I don't have to leave. I haven't done anything wrong. She was coming on to me."

"I asked you nicely, now please leave," said Brian. Instead of walking away, Paul decided to take a drunken swing at Brian. Brian stopped him easily and promptly cuffed him.

"That was stupid," said Brian. "Also, you are under arrest." There were murmurs and a few whistles of approval from the bar crowd around them, and Paul sneered in response. Patricia was confused and sat down on the bar stool, taking it all in.

# chapter fourteen

Patricia sat at the bar and watched Brian read Paul his Miranda rights. She absently picked up her drink. Brian saw her and grabbed the glass away from her.

"What are you doing?" asked Patricia.

"Did you watch that drink the whole time? Or did he order it when you weren't looking? He could have drugged that drink," said Brian. Patricia looked at him in shock. She was still tipsy but thought back carefully. Sure enough, she remembered that Paul had ordered the drink while she was in the restroom. Another officer came into the bar.

"Officer Sims, please get him out of here. The charge is assaulting a police officer. And, hang on a second." Officer Sims held Paul still while Brian patted down the man's pockets. He reached into Paul's jacket pocket and pulled out a little baggie of unmarked pills. "What's this? Looks like rohypnol to me," Brian said. "Roofies. Do you have a prescription for this, sir?" His tone was stern but controlled. Paul was silent.

Patricia opened her mouth, but no words came out. She was in shock. The other officer took Paul away. The nearby bar patrons gave them a wide berth. Patricia had no intention of staying there any longer. She stepped out onto the sidewalk and Brian followed her.

She felt the buzz of alcohol in her veins competing with adrenaline from the near-miss with the sleazy Paul. She was also filled with questions. Before Brian could say anything, she turned to face him, and everything spilled out. "What are you doing here? Where have you been all day? I called and texted you so many times! I got assaulted after our date and ended up in the hospital with a concussion. Now I'm just trying to enjoy myself and you show up to save me? Why are you even here?" She stopped, breath heaving in her lungs.

"Patricia, what are you talking about? You told me to meet you here."

"What?" Her eyes popped wide. She was pretty sure she would have remembered doing that.

"Yes. You called me about an hour ago. All you said was, 'Take me to that skull bar in Little Five Points'. You sounded pretty drunk and hung up on me. I was really worried. I was out patrolling with Officer Sims at the time and we drove here as fast as possible."

Patricia was flabbergasted. She dug her phone out of her purse and checked the call log. Sure enough, she had pocket-dialled Brian right when she stepped into the taxi. It all became clear. She realized what had happened.

Patricia looked up at him and burst into laughter. She laughed so hard that she swayed on her feet and tears leaked down her cheeks.

Brian looked at her in confusion. Finally, he steadied her by the arm and they walked down the sidewalk. "Come on. I know a nearby diner. It looks like you could use some coffee," he said.

The diner was clean and bright. It reminded Patricia of a small diner she had been to outside of New York. The waitress knew Brian by name and brought them each a big mug of hot coffee. Brian ordered her a stack of pancakes. "It will help absorb the alcohol," he explained.

She gratefully ate the food and Patricia started to sober up. "How does the waitress know you?" she asked.

"I come here all the time. I discovered it early on and have been coming back for a long time. They've got the best coffee in the city," said Brian. "It's not much, but it's cozy."

Patricia glanced around at the red vinyl booths and the round chrome stools at the front counter. "It's nice. It feels like…home." Patricia looked at him as she said this and realized the diner was nice, but it was also the company that made it feel so wonderful in that moment.

"I am so sorry I couldn't come to the hospital," said Brian to break the silence. "I was worried sick when I found out. You'll never believe what happened the night after our date."

It thrilled her to hear him describe it as a date, too. "Something to do with the case?"

"I was alerted that Jeff Jones booked a plane ticket to Amsterdam. He was planning to flee the country. I had to get a warrant for his arrest and search his house immediately, which meant I had to wake up the county judge who oversees warrants for our jurisdiction and…well, it's a long, boring story, but the point is that I couldn't get away. I spent all night getting the warrants and then tracking down Jeff Jones before he could get on the plane."

Patricia was amazed. "He sounds pretty guilty. Did he confess?"

"No. He claimed he was just going to Amsterdam to do some international banking. Before he could produce any evidence to corroborate his story, his lawyer stepped in and got him released on bail. He can't leave the country. We don't have any concrete evidence to tie him to the crime," said Brian.

"Wow. What about Hannah Sedgewick? Did you interview her again yet?"

"Not yet. I plan to interview her again soon. I learned a few things about her when I was chasing down leads all day on those warrants. I also tracked down Peter Sedgewick's business banking records from Imperial Capital. There wasn't a lot there, however."

Patricia heard Brian's frustration. "It seems like so many of these leads are turning up empty."

"That just means that someone isn't telling us the truth." He paused and looked at her. "Speaking of the truth…Tom and Valerie finally got ahold of me. They read me the riot act for not coming to the hospital. And for not being honest about your involvement in the investigation."

"I am an awful friend," said Patricia, burying her head in her hands. "I should not have lied to them."

"No, you are not an awful friend," said Brian. "You were right to keep things quiet. I'm not sure why Tom was so darn protective of you. He really is convinced there's a killer out in the woods, even though we have no evidence that this was a random murder. They told me about your RV getting vandalized. I feel sick about what happened, and I can only imagine how you are feeling."

Patricia's eyes welled up. She thought about her beautiful little RV again, covered in that ugly red paint, then put her face in her palm and wept for a few minutes. Brian got up and moved next to Patricia. He held her in his arms while she cried.

"I don't know what I'm going to do. That RV is my life," Patricia sobbed. "It's my only home."

"We'll figure something out," said Brian. He rubbed a warm palm over her shoulders. "Listen, it's late. Why don't you come back to my place? You can have my bed and I will sleep on the sofa. You can't go back to your RV when it's all marked up like that. I feel rotten, it's my fault," said Brian.

"Why would it be your fault?" asked Patricia.

"Because I let you help with the investigation," said Brian. "And then I didn't make sure you got safely into your RV that night. Also, if I'd been the officer on the scene, I would have posted a guard, and nobody would have come creeping around with spray paint, that's for sure."

Patricia smiled at his fierce insistence. "Well, I insisted on helping with the investigation," said Patricia. "None of it is your fault." She leaned on Brian's shoulder and sighed. "I will take you up on your offer," said Patricia, "although I'll take the sofa."

"Absolutely not," said Brian instantly. "I insist you take the bed."

Patricia felt safe nestled into Brian's shoulder. She did not want to argue about it anymore. "Okay," she said.

They took a cab back to Brian's truck and then drove out towards east Atlanta. Brian had a small house in Decatur. It was a cute, two-story brick house. The yard sloped down the front of the house and the drive circled around to the back. Brian had a hedge bordering his property on both sides which gave him some privacy from his neighbors. It was a beautiful house.

"I know this neighborhood," said Patricia happily. On her first days exploring Atlanta, the bus had passed near here and she had admired the well-kept gardens and beautiful houses. "I love this part of town."

"Hey, what do you know? So do I," said Brian. Patricia laughed. She walked up the couple steps to Brian's front door. There was barking inside. Patricia smiled.

"I forgot to tell you about my dog. Are you okay with dogs?" asked Brian.

"Yes, I am," said Patricia. They were met at the door by a black Labrador who jumped up to greet Brian and then sniffed at Patricia's hand.

"Her name is Belle," said Brian.

"She is beautiful," said Patricia, stroking Belle's fur. Belle sat and wagged her tail.

"She likes you," said Brian. Patricia smiled. Brian showed her his bedroom and gave her some sweats to change into. He made her drink a big glass of water and take some ibuprofen —just enough to help prevent a hangover in the morning, he promised. He said goodnight and shut the door.

Patricia changed and laid down. She was a little self-conscious and listened to the sounds of Brian settling in to sleep in the living room. She felt so much better. Safe and warm, Patricia snuggled under the covers and went to sleep.

The next morning, Patricia was awoken by a wet nose and a sloppy kiss.

"Bella," she heard Brian call. "Get out of there, girl."

Patricia laughed. The Labrador leaped down from the bed and trotted back out of the room. Patricia got up and went into the kitchen. There was sun streaming in from a bay window. On the wall were some bookshelves with cookbooks. A breakfast nook divided the kitchen and the living room. Belle greeted Patricia again and quickly obeyed when she told the beautiful dog to sit. Brian had eggs and coffee waiting for her at the table in the breakfast nook. Patricia thanked him and sat down.

Brian joined her at the table. He gave her a warm smile and asked lots of questions about her headache. He seemed satisfied that her concussion was not turning into anything serious, however.

"You never told me what you found out about Hannah," she said to Brian.

"Well, I thought about another angle. I thought she might have killed Peter to inherit his business," said Brian. "It turns out that Hannah has her own money. She has no need of Peter's inheritance."

"Okay, so she is ruled out," said Patricia.

"Not completely, but her alibi checked out," said Brian.

"So who's next?" asked Patricia.

"Lana," said Brian. "I think she knows more about Jeff. We need to get all the information possible before we confront him again. If he was truly involved in the murder, and he has such a good lawyer, we will probably only get one more chance to interrogate him. It has to count."

"We?" asked Patricia hopefully.

"I definitely want you there," said Brian with a smile. "After what happened the other night at your RV, I am not letting you out of my sight until this case is solved."

Patricia felt a thrill inside. Just then, her phone buzzed in her purse. She reached over to check it.

"Is that Tom and Valerie checking up on you again?"

Patricia read it carefully. Lenore had texted her the date and time for her flight to Paris. She realized with a start that there were only two days left before her flight. She was not sure how to tell Brian. "No, just something from my publisher," she said vaguely.

"Are you ready to come with me to interview Lana?" he asked. Patricia decided she would enjoy the thrill of the investigation for one more day before telling him.

"Let's go," she said with a big smile.

# chapter fifteen

Lana Morris looked surprised to see Brian and Patricia when they stepped off the elevator, but she quickly recovered her composure.

"Officer Johnson. Are you here to see Jeff? I'm sorry to say that he's out sick today," Lana said.

"Actually, we are here to see you. Do you have time for a few questions?" Brian asked. If Lana knew that her boss had been detained on suspicion of murder, she said nothing. *Maybe that's why Jeff is not here today,* thought Patricia. *Too many people with too many questions.*

Once again, Lana set her phone on auto-answer and led them to the conference room down the hall. She nervously clutched at a tissue when she sat down. Patricia noticed that she seemed steadier than she had during the first meeting.

"Ms. Morris, I have reason to believe you did not tell us the whole truth last time," said Brian. Lana immediately blushed and looked away.

"I told you everything, Detective," she said in a quiet voice.

"Would the two gentlemen from the Foxtrot Club say the same thing?" he asked in a blunt tone. Lana's face paled.

"How do you know about that?"

"Ms. Morris, we followed you that night. We overheard a number of interesting things. It is in your best interest to tell us what you know," Brian said.

Lana turned the tissue over in her hands again and again. She was silent for a moment. "I don't want Jeff to get in trouble…"

"Which Jeff would that be?"

She looked at them with embarrassment. "My boss, I mean. You followed me to my boyfriend's DJ night at the other club, too?" Brian nodded, and she looked down at her hands. Finally, Lana sighed. "Fine. Mr. Jones told me to keep quiet about this, but it seems like I have no secrets left. I saw Hannah and Peter Sedgewick have a huge blow-up of a fight here in the office. It was early in the evening before he was found dead."

Patricia and Brian exchanged a meaningful look. It was dead silent in the room. "Lana, any detail you can give us about that night will help the investigation."

"I only saw the start of the fight. I was getting ready to leave for the day when Hannah arrived with some papers. She looked livid. I thought she was going to chew me out at first. But she headed for her husband's office and started yelling at him. Screaming in rage." Lana shook her head as if the memory still scared her. "I couldn't hear the exact words. As they argued, Peter tried to walk away from her, and she followed him. They were moving towards my desk and I didn't know what to do—should I leave, should I pretend not to hear? Then Jeff came running out, took one look at Hannah, and practically shoved me in the elevator. He said to forget I'd seen anything. I didn't think anything of it…of course I'm not a gossip…but then the next day when the news came out about Peter…" Lana's lower lip trembled again and tears threatened to take over.

"It's okay, take your time," said Patricia gently.

"When the news came about Peter's death, Jeff came to me and said we both had to keep that fight quiet. As a favor to Mrs. Sedgewick. I couldn't stand the thought of doing her any favors, but I did it for Peter's sake. In memory of him," she finished sadly. "Was I wrong? Am I in trouble?"

"Lana, your boss instructed you to lie to the authorities. That's not on you, that's on him," Brian said. Lana nodded in relief. "The important thing is that you told us the truth today."

Brian asked her if she saw what papers Hannah Sedgewick had been carrying that day, but she didn't recall any details. They thanked Lana and said goodbye. When they were back in Brian's truck, they discussed what they had just learned. "Wow. It seems like Mrs. Sedgewick has an anger problem," Patricia commented.

Brian looked skeptical. "Maybe she and Jeff both have something to hide. We have to get her side of the story." They drove to the Sedgewick house to confront Hannah.

The Sedgewick house was just as elegant and massive as Patricia remembered it. When Brian parked in the driveway, they saw a florist's van leaving by a back entrance. Nearby several funeral wreaths were being loaded into Hannah's car. "I think we got here just in time," Brian said. "Looks like she's headed out to set up flowers at the memorial."

"I feel bad pressing her with more questions this close to the funeral," said Patricia.

Brian nodded as they walked up to the front door. "I have the same thought sometimes during these hard investigations. But then I remind myself it's better than the alternative. What if you play it too safe and the real killer gets away?"

Patricia gulped. Hannah's maid Lilith answered the door

and once more showed them into the tastefully appointed living room. Mrs. Sedgewick was waiting there for them, an impatient look on her face.

"Detective Johnson. I was not expecting you today. Has there been a development in the investigation?"

"We are working on several leads," Brian replied. Patricia's heart raced. Hannah had no idea what was coming. Or perhaps she did and was playing Brian for a fool. "Some new information has come to light and I need to ask you a few questions."

"Of course," said the woman. She gracefully swept back a lock of her blonde hair and crossed her long, tan legs demurely at the ankle. Patricia noticed she was still wearing black, another perfectly tailored dress.

Brian opened his notepad and consulted his notes briefly. He took his time and Patricia wondered if he was doing it to make Mrs. Sedgewick impatient. "On the night of Peter's death, we have a witness who says you were at his office building." He looked up at her expectantly.

"I told you, I was at my book club that evening," she replied, dismissing the idea.

"Our witness says there was a dramatic, perhaps violent confrontation between you and your husband," Brian stated calmly. "Your book club didn't start until later that night. We have your alibi for the time of the murder. You do not have an alibi for the time of the confrontation, however. What happened at his office that evening?"

Hannah's eyes flashed. "This is absurd," she said. "Jeff promised me—" she broke off and looked deeply uncomfortable.

"What did Jeff Jones promise you?" Brian prompted.

She seemed to realize it was too late to take back her slip of the tongue. "He promised me he would keep that quiet. He said their little secretary wouldn't blab about it, either. I guess he lied. Perhaps I should have expected that," she said bitterly. "Yes, there was a confrontation that night. I went to my husband's office to confront him because he was having an affair. I did not tell you this before because...well, because he promised me that night he would end it. Once and for all. I believed him, too." She looked away from Brian and Patricia and an embarrassed flush rose on her cheeks. "I had received an anonymous letter in the mail that afternoon telling me that Peter was having an affair with that awful woman—there were photographs—and I flew into a terrible rage. I knew what it meant for his business. I knew what it meant for us. I drove to his office building to confront him."

"What happened?"

"I told him I had proof. He demanded to know how I had gotten the pictures. I told him it didn't matter, he simply needed to end the affair. I...I made some threats I'm not proud of." She paused and did not look up. "I told him I would leak the news to the gossip columns myself if he didn't end it."

"So, your threat worked? He agreed to stop the affair?"

"You make me sound so awful. I wasn't going to go through with it! And anyway, Jeff stepped in. He seemed oddly frantic about the whole thing. He begged Peter to see the sense of things, to not ruin his life like he almost had all those years ago with his drug problem. He begged me not to take the pictures to the press. Eventually, Peter broke down crying. He promised he would end it. He loved me. He said the affair didn't mean anything—it was simply blowing off steam, a stress relief—he didn't love that woman. Whoever told you the confrontation was violent...they were wrong. It may have started out pretty loud, but by the time it was over, my husband and I were in tears and in each other's arms. Peter said he would go and break it off with the other woman that very night. And that was that."

"What happened to the pictures?" Brian said.

"Jeff burnt the pictures in an old ashtray and vowed he would help us track down the blackmailer," she said. "He was very concerned about the blackmailer." Hannah sighed and looked miserable. Patricia was disappointed. Surely the pictures would have been a helpful clue.

"Then what happened?"

"I went to my book club after that, as I told you. I was fully expecting him to come home afterward and tell me he had broken it off with that horrible woman. But he…he never came home." She broke down in tears again.

"Mrs. Sedgewick, I know this is difficult to talk about, but can you describe the woman in the pictures?" Brian said. "We can bring in a sketch artist—"

Hannah's head snapped up angrily. "You don't need a sketch artist. I can tell you her name. It's Susan Hendron. She works in downtown Atlanta."

After they left the Sedgewick home, Patricia's head was spinning, and it was not from her fading concussion. "Do you think Susan had something to do with the murder?" she asked Brian.

Brian shook his head. "Remember the day she came into Peter's office looking for him? She was shocked by the news."

Patricia remembered Ms. Hendron's reaction that day, as clear as a bell. Then she thought for a moment. "Brian, something bothered me about what Hannah said. Did you notice she used the word 'blackmail' about how Jeff Jones reacted to the photos? It sounded as if that was Jeff's worry more than it was Hannah's or Peter's. Hannah had the pictures but didn't say she would leak them. Peter wasn't worried about the pictures, he was worried about his marriage. So why did Jeff Jones start worrying about a blackmailer all of a sudden?"

"She also said that he burnt them personally, instead of turning them over to the police. I think you're right, Patricia. We have to get him to talk to us about those pictures."

# chapter sixteen

Brian was worried that as soon as they approached Jeff Jones for another interview, he would clam up and call his lawyer. He asked Patricia if she was willing to help with a little ruse. She readily agreed.

Patricia called Jeff Jones that afternoon from Brian's office.

"Hello, Mr. Jones? This is Patricia. I don't know if you remember me. I'm Detective Johnson's assistant." She tried to make her voice sound timid. Brian nodded encouragingly as he listened to her phone call from across the desk.

"Of course, I remember you," Jeff answered in a guarded voice. "How can I help you?"

"Well, sir, this is very embarrassing, but I'm hoping you can do me a favor. I lost my boss's notes from when we interviewed you at your office. I can't lose my job over this..."

"I understand," he said in a charming voice. "I'd be happy to answer the questions again. My schedule is a little busy this afternoon, but I can meet you early this evening?" He named a chic downtown seafood restaurant and Patricia agreed to meet him there.

"Thank you so much, Mr. Jones." They hung up. Patricia's heart was beating out of her chest and she grinned at Brian. He gave her a huge thumbs-up.

"You did great," he said.

The restaurant was a seafood place by an historic cemetery. The décor was designed so the patrons felt like they were in the ocean. Patricia wore a light linen suit with a slightly low-cut silk blouse. Brian had scowled a little when she picked it out, but he agreed that it might help their gambit. She saw Jeff at the bar when she walked in. Patricia was glad when Jeff suggested a table near the windows at the front of the restaurant.

"Hello again," said Jeff, shaking Patricia's hand. He held out the chair for Patricia and she thanked him.

"Good evening," Patricia said. "Thank you so much again, Mr. Jones." The waitress came over and they both ordered iced tea. Jeff suggested an appetizer and Patricia agreed. The waitress left.

"Please, call me Jeff."

"This will be a huge help. I brought my follow-up questions," Patricia said, leaning forward to pull a steno notebook and pen from her purse. "Promise you won't tell my boss?" She smiled sweetly at him.

He smiled back at her. "Of course. Now, what questions do you need to review?" asked Jeff.

The waitress came back with their appetizer and two plates. The appetizer was grilled alligator bites. "Have you had alligator before?" asked Jeff.

"No, but I am always willing to try something new," said Patricia. She took a bite. It tasted like gamey chicken, but she played along.

"Yum," said Patricia. "This is so swanky. We could have just met in your office, Jeff."

"And pass up the chance to take a pretty lady out to a nice restaurant? Please." He gave her another charming grin. Over more bites of the appetizer, Patricia got down to business.

"My boss has me writing up a report on Mr. Sedgewick's life. Background profile stuff. Your interview was so helpful for that. I'm so sorry for your loss…but can you tell me when you met Peter?" Patricia asked.

"Yes," said Jeff. "We knew each other in college. After we graduated from Duke University, we both moved here. We had always wanted to work in the same field, though he was very ambitious and wanted to start his own business. I was worried about his partying habits."

"That's right, he went to rehab at some point?" said Patricia.

"Yes. I thought Hannah would have told you all about this."

"We are trying to respect her privacy during this difficult time," Patricia lied, crossing her fingers in her lap under the tablecloth. "You helped him get his job, correct?"

"That's right. When he came back from rehab, his business venture had fallen apart, but he was back on the straight and narrow. I got him a job at the same company as me. He started only a month or so after I did," he said.

"Did you know Hannah in college too?" she asked.

"No, she did not go to school with us. He met Hannah here in Atlanta," said Jeff. "I actually set them up."

"You did? How did that happen?" Patricia asked.

"Well, Hannah was a friend of mine. She moved in high society circles and my father knew her father through their country club. She would sometimes come to the office and hang out with me at lunch. One day, Peter joined us. After lunch that day, Hannah hounded me until I set her up on a date with Peter. The rest, as they say, was history," said Jeff with a fond grin.

"How would you describe Hannah and Peter's relationship?" asked Patricia.

"They were very much in love. You know how people talk about a power couple? That was the Sedgewicks. Hannah pushed Peter to be his very best. Peter loved the challenge. He loved Hannah," said Jeff.

"Do you think she ever pushed him too far?" asked Patricia. She didn't look him in the eye as she asked it, merely concentrated on scribbling down her answers.

He paused. "I don't think so, no. Anything she asked of him, it all came from a place of love."

This was it. Time for the hard part. Patricia took a deep breath. "Would you say Hannah asked Peter to end his affair with Susan because of love, too? Or because the photos you took caused her to fly into a jealous rage?"

There was an awkward silence. Jeff Jones was staring at her and he was red in the face. "What do you think you're doing?" he said.

Patricia looked as innocent as she could manage. It was a gamble and a white lie, but it was necessary to get him to talk about the blackmail angle. "Yes, the photos you took and sent to Hannah…she told us all about them."

Jeff did not reply. He merely stood up and dropped his napkin onto his plate, then dropped a couple twenties onto the table and stormed out of the restaurant.

Patricia spoke into the wire hidden in her blouse. "Brian, can you hear me? He left. He just walked out. We're going to lose him." She stood up and followed him to the door, unsure what to do. She tried not to panic. Their plan had not worked.

# chapter seventeen

On the sidewalk, Patricia was relieved to see Brian walking up to confront Jeff before he could get very far. The tall detective blocked Jeff's path on the sidewalk with one hand. Jeff gave Brian an angry look.

"Detective Johnson, what is the meaning of this? This is an ambush. This is entrapment. My lawyer will—"

"Your lawyer will find it very difficult to get you a good plea deal if you don't explain to me right now why I shouldn't arrest you for blackmail."

Jeff stilled. "Blackmail?" There was a long, quiet pause. The city around them was hushed in the early evening light. "You think that's what I was trying to do?"

Brian and Patricia waited.

"That's absurd. No. I was trying to protect her. I just wanted her back. I wanted Peter to do the right thing."

"Protect who, Mr. Jones?" Patricia asked carefully.

"Susan. The love of my life." His voice broke a little as he said it. He looked at Patricia and said, "Tell me this, have you ever been in love with someone who didn't feel the same way towards you?" Patricia found herself blushing. She did not look over at Brian.

"Yes."

"You know that feeling where you will do anything to make them notice you?" He sighed.

"Mr. Jones, would you kill for Susan?" Brian asked in a quiet voice.

"No! No. I just sent the letter and the photos to Hannah to…to get things in motion, I guess. I never intended to hurt anyone. I had no idea Hannah would fly off the handle about the pictures. I just wanted Peter to go back to his loving wife, and for Susan to get out of that messy situation. And then maybe…maybe Susan might turn to me for comfort." He paused and looked at Brian with a wry look. "Blackmail, eh? I can see now why you thought I was fleeing to Amsterdam."

"It did look very suspicious," Brian said.

Jeff rolled his eyes. "I'll show you my uncle's will if you want. I received a letter from his solicitor in Amsterdam last week. I have to sign in person to collect the check from his estate. Bad timing, perhaps, but I'm not guilty of anything except being foolish when it comes to Susan."

"Did Peter know you were in love with her?" Brian asked.

"No. But those photos…I was worried he would realize I was the only one who knew where they were the night they were taken. What if he guessed and told her I did it? I burnt them at the first opportunity. Susan could never know."

"Why does it matter if she sees them? She was there. She knows what happened."

"Don't you get it?" Jeff spat bitterly. "I've been in love with her for years. Ever since we met in college. Susan never felt the same way. Then she was swept off her feet by Peter… my married, best friend Peter. She deserves so much better. She deserves to be a queen, not some secret girlfriend hiding in a hotel."

"Why should we believe that you did not kill Peter?" asked Patricia. "You wanted to be with Susan. That could only happen with Peter out of the way."

"I see where you might think that," said Jeff. "Honestly, I

would doubt me, too. After the confrontation at the office, I was supposed to drive Peter to Susan's house, but I was a wreck. I drove him partway there and then made my excuses and he said he would walk the rest of the way there. Then I drove to Cobb County to my mother's house. You can check out my alibi with her. I stayed the night."

"I will check that out," said Brian. Patricia thought that Jeff did seem heartbroken about Susan. He was a man lost in grief and heartbreak, not a man who had lashed out violently at his best friend. Patricia could imagine Jeff holding in his feelings all of those years. *Unrequited love is so sad,* Patricia thought.

"Maybe I took the coward's way out by sending those photos," said Jeff. "I have felt sick with guilt ever since Peter's death, knowing that I played a part in his last evening alive."

Brian made a motion as if he was ready to leave, but Patricia felt sure there was more to the story. "You say you were in love with Susan since college…did Peter know her then, too?" Patricia asked.

"Yes. They were serious for a couple years. Peter admitted to me that they were unofficially engaged at one point. He broke it off with her at one point and she almost lost her mind —trashed his apartment, spray-painted awful things on his car. She was a little wild," Jeff chuckled. "But weren't we all, in college? Love is like that." His expression turned somber again. "Anyway, they figured it out, got back together, and were a very sweet couple for a while after that. Then she broke it off with Peter for good, just before graduation. It broke his heart. That was one of the reasons he moved to Atlanta when I did. He wanted to be far away from Susan. He still had feelings for her. He needed a distraction," said Jeff.

"When did they start this affair?" asked Patricia.

"Well, one day she showed up at the office. I thought I was dreaming. She only had eyes for him. She said she just happened to get a job in Atlanta. Peter and Hannah had been married for over ten years at that point. It knocked Peter for a loop, too," said Jeff.

"What happened?" asked Patricia.

"I think they went out to lunch. After that, I saw them around town a few times, at lunch, once or twice in a nice restaurant for dinner. He always downplayed it, claimed it was just a friendship. He said he loved his wife and that I had nothing to worry about."

"Did you believe him?" asked Patricia.

"At first. But then one night I needed to find him to ask a question about work. Someone said they saw him go into a club with Lana from work. He was always trying to help Lana network. When I went to the club, I found him but then he went back to his table and he wasn't with Lana—he was with Susan. He thought I left but I watched them from across the club. I saw how she looked at him. It killed me that he was lying about it to everyone, not just to me, but to his wife," said Jeff. He looked embarrassed. "That night I followed them to a hotel."

"Where you took the pictures?" Brian asked Jeff.

"It wasn't anything indecent. I just took pictures of them kissing in the hotel bar, and later in the hot tub outside by the hotel pool."

"That was proof enough for you?" Brian sounded skeptical.

Jeff snorted. "Do you kiss your friends in hot tubs? If you had a wife, would she like it if you did? Sorry, Detective, I don't mean to be flippant. I saw how Peter reacted when Hannah came storming in that night. He knew his goose was cooked. I thought I would be glad when the truth came out…but I didn't feel happy about it, not one bit. All I could picture was how Susan would react. Hannah had those pictures in her hand and I just… panicked. That's partly why I drove to my mother's that night. I knew if Peter told Susan my photos were the cause of their break-up, she would probably want revenge in the worst way."

"Do you believe he really went to see Susan Hendron as he promised?" Patricia asked Jeff. "Is there any chance he went somewhere else that night?"

"No. He definitely went to her house. He even texted me when he got there," said Jeff.

"Why?" asked Patricia.

"Because I had dropped him off in her neighborhood, but also, I suppose, because he wanted to make it official. It had been such a crazy night." He pulled out his phone and scrolled through the messages to show them. *Thanks for everything. You're a true friend, Jeff. I'm at her place now and I'm going to make this right,* his message read. "That was the last I heard from him."

"Do you think Susan Hendron could have killed Peter Sedgewick?" Brian asked.

Jeff was looking down at his feet. Reluctantly, he looked up at the detective. "Are you asking me if the love of my life is a murderer?" He paused and took a breath. "I've been scared to even think that thought since Peter was found dead, Detective. I…I can't answer that question. Please don't make me answer it." He looked down again, ashamed.

Brian looked at Patricia. "Are you thinking what I'm thinking?"

"Yes. We have to find Susan." Patricia turned to Jeff. "Thank you for your honesty. I know this has been a painful time for you." She felt sympathy for the poor man. Despite his poor choices, he had been motivated by a sincere desire to help the woman he loved. She hoped he would find love one day.

However, there was no time to dwell on the tragedy of it all. Brian grabbed Patricia's hand and they practically ran to the truck.

"I need to call in an All Points Bulletin for Susan

Hendron," Brian said into his radio. Patricia had a sudden thought.

"Brian, I know where we can find Susan."

"What? How?"

"Do you have a tuxedo ready? Tonight we're going to rub elbows with Atlanta's elite." Brian grinned, intrigued. He drove her back to the campground so she could get changed. She laughed and promised to tell him her secret when he picked her up that evening.

# chapter eighteen

"I am glad I shopped at Sax Fifth Avenue when I was in New York last month," Patricia said to Valerie when she was back in her RV. She opened the garment bag hanging in her closet to reveal the special dress she had purchased on sale. Valerie gasped.

The emerald green cocktail dress fell in a gentle drape of satiny fabric. Little cap sleeves accentuated the rounded neckline and princess seams ran down to the fitted waist. The knee-length dress fit her like a dream, and she was thrilled to finally have the perfect occasion to wear it.

"You are going to look incredible. What time is Brian picking you up?" Valerie said.

"I think seven."

"We've got plenty of time. Can I do your hair and makeup, please?" Valerie's eyes shone with excitement and Patricia could not help but laugh.

"Okay. I guess this is worth the effort. It is one of the nicest restaurants in Atlanta. I'm excited to add it to my article." Her hair was freshly washed, and she wore a t-shirt and jeans while Valerie got to work.

Patricia was happy that Valerie was an ace at taming her wild red curls. There was no mirror in the main living space where they worked, so she could not see the final effect quite yet.

When she was done with Patricia's hair, Valerie told her to stay in the chair.

"It is makeup time," Valerie declared. "But first, when was your last manicure?"

"Never," Patricia laughed. "I do my own nails."

"Well, you are getting one today," Valerie declared. She dunked Patricia's nails in a soapy solution and went back to her RV to fetch a bag of her emery boards and other nail supplies. She picked out a pretty shade of nail polish that was subtle yet sexy. Patricia was impressed. While her nails dried, Valerie applied Patricia's makeup.

"If you don't like it, you will have time to take it off and do it yourself before Brian gets here," Valerie reassured Patricia. She put on the finishing touches and finally let Patricia see herself in a mirror. Patricia's mouth gaped open.

"You don't like it," said Valerie, a bit dejectedly. "Tom said I should just stick to hair."

"Valerie, I love it," said Patricia. Valerie squealed with happiness.

"You really like it?" Valerie asked.

"Yes, I do," said Patricia. Valerie had brought out Patricia's green eyes and high cheekbones. Patricia could not believe what Valerie had done with her hair. Valerie had straightened the wild curls into loose waves and used bobby pins to twist it back from one side of Patricia's face. Her hair softly framed her face.

"I look like a Hollywood star," said Patricia.

"Yes, you do," said Valerie. Patricia carefully hugged Valerie and thanked her. When she helped Valerie carry all the supplies back to the couples' RV, Tom whistled.

"Wow, you look gorgeous," he said to Patricia.

"Never doubt your wife's abilities again," Patricia chided him.

"I won't," Tom promised. Patricia walked back to her RV with a spring in her step. It was easy to ignore the red paint on her RV. As a surprise for her, Tom had draped the side of her RV with a clean tarp so that she didn't have to look at it or deal with it until she was ready.

She put on the emerald green dress. She put on a new pair of high-heeled sandals in pale pink with delicate ankle straps. Patricia felt like a princess. Now all she needed was her prince.

A few minutes later, Brian pulled up in his truck. Patricia heard him and went outside. Brian stopped dead in his tracks.

"Wow," he said. Brian had on a grey designer suit with narrow lapels and a sapphire blue bowtie that matched his eyes.

"Wow to you, too," said Patricia.

"I like going out on stakeouts with you," said Brian. Patricia laughed. Brian gently helped her into the truck. When he climbed into his seat next to her, he stared at her for a moment longer. Her heart fluttered.

"What?" she asked nervously.

"Nothing. You're just beautiful. The best lucky charm a guy could wish for," he said. She blushed, remembering how he had joked about that when they first met.

Valerie and Tom waved as they drove by their RV. Brian and Patricia waved back.

"Now, would you mind telling me where we are going tonight?" Brian asked. Patricia told him how she had seen the dinner date on Peter Sedgewick's appointment calendar and remembered Jeff Jones mentioned a place he had seen Peter and Susan together, too. She told him it was Aria, and Brian whistled.

"Okay," he said. He put the address into his GPS and started driving.

"Will we be able to get in?" asked Patricia.

"I'll talk to the person in the front and let them know what's going on. It won't be a problem," Brian said.

"What a great job perk," said Patricia.

Brian agreed. "Maybe we should have all our dates on stakeouts," he teased her. They drove up to North Atlanta. When they got to their destination, Brian drove the truck to the valet.

"When in Rome…" Brian said. Patricia giggled. The uniformed valet attendant helped Patricia out of the car. Brian came around and took her hand. He handed the keys to the attendant and put her hand in the crook of his arm and they walked towards the restaurant. Large black letters spelled out *ARIA* against the white wall of the restaurant. It was tasteful and understated. Brian and Patricia entered the black doors and walked into a fairy tale. At least, that was what Patricia was thinking. The tables were draped with white cloths and set with crystal glasses for each guest. A black and white floral wallpaper accented the room and the art deco style chandelier reminded Patricia of shooting stars.

There were statues of animals under arches at the far side of the room. Across the way, there were bay windows overlooking a beautiful lake surrounded by trees. Beside a wall draped with white curtains was the bar. Patricia nudged Brian and pointed out the marble-topped bar with every imaginable liquor. Sitting at the bar was Susan Hendron.

Brian and Patricia sat down at the other end of the bar. Susan Hendron was wearing a silky white dress and did not seem to notice them. She had her blonde hair pulled back in a chignon and she was carrying a small sequined clutch purse. Despite her stunning outfit and immaculate looks, Susan was distraught. She slouched a little against the bar as she finished her mixed drink.

While they were watching Susan, a waiter came over to her. She nodded and followed him to a table set for two. Susan sat down, and the waiter brought her another drink. At one point, the waiter walked past Brian. Brian caught the waiter's attention and discreetly flashed his badge.

"Can you tell me if you have seen that woman here before?" Brian asked the waiter while motioning towards Susan.

"Oh yes," said the waiter. "She comes here every few weeks."

"Does she dine alone?" asked Brian.

"No. She is usually with Mr. Sedgewick." Here the waiter bowed his head. When he lifted it back up his eyes were moist. "Mr. Sedgewick was one of our best customers. That was his table. He had a standing reservation here," the waiter said. Across the room the floor manager motioned to the waiter.

"I have to go," said the waiter. Brian thanked him and tipped him. Patricia put her hand on Brian's arm and nodded towards Susan. Susan was sitting with her face in her hands. Her drink was empty—evidently she had drunk it down rather quickly. Her shoulders were shaking as if she was crying. The other restaurant patrons were doing their best to ignore her, but it was obviously difficult. Her sobs became louder and the waitstaff began to look alarmed.

"Let's go over and talk to her," Patricia suggested. "We can't just leave her alone like this."

"Okay, but let's be cautious," said Brian. They walked over to Susan's table and Patricia sat beside her. Patricia could tell that Susan was quite tipsy.

"Hello, Susan," said Patricia, putting her hand on Susan's arm.

Susan looked up. She tried to compose herself. "Who are you?" Susan asked.

"I am Patricia. I met you outside of Peter's office the other day, do you remember? This is Detective Johnson," said Patricia, motioning to Brian who stood a careful distance away.

"I remember," said Susan, nodding vaguely.

"We spoke to Jeff Jones. He gave us some information about the investigation and it's urgent that we talk to you about it," said Patricia gently.

The woman's eyes filled up with tears again. A look of bitter rage flitted across her features and she wiped hastily at her eyes. She started speaking quickly, babbling angry words that Patricia could just barely make out. "Jeff…that backstabber…he knew—" Her voice grew in volume and the maître d' gave Brian a look of alarm from across the room. Brian quickly stepped in.

"Ms. Hendron, please, won't you allow us to help you?" said the Detective, grasping her arm gently but firmly and helping her to stand. As she stood up, Susan snatched a large glass of white wine from her table. Together they escorted the distraught woman to the cool, quiet hallway by the restrooms.

Susan muttered angry words in between gulps of wine. She shot a poisonous look at the maître d' and the waiters.

"Susan, I hate to see you suffer like this," said Patricia. "Will you let us help you get home? Perhaps you'll be more comfortable there and we can go over some of the questions we have."

Susan sniffed and looked lost. Then she turned and looked at Patricia. "Yes," Susan said with decision. "Once we get there, I'll tell you all about that traitor, Jeff," she spat. She downed the last of her wine in one swallow. Brian grimaced, realizing her blood alcohol level must be dangerously high at this point. He stepped forward and took Susan's keys from her purse and said he would drive Susan back to her place. Susan hesitated, but then agreed. Patricia would drive Brian's truck to follow them.

While Susan went to get her coat, Brian gave Patricia his valet ticket. Patricia, Brian, and Susan walked to the front of the restaurant. Susan swayed a little on her feet and continued to dab angrily at her tears. The valets brought Brian's truck around for Patricia and then Susan's Mercedes convertible drove up. It was sleek and silver. Brian helped Susan climb in and then got in the driver's seat. He pulled ahead of Patricia and she followed him towards upper Atlanta.

They wound through traffic and ended up in the Buckhead area. Patricia followed Brian down a small street. He stopped and parked by a large condominium. Patricia was glad to see the street and the neighborhood were well-lit and bright. Despite the late hour, she saw a man taking a cute dog on an evening walk.

"Her apartment is bigger than my first house," Patricia gawked. She parked Brian's truck behind the convertible. Brian helped Susan out of the truck. Patricia took Susan's keys from her sparkly purse and unlocked the front door. Susan swayed on her feet again, then led the way into her apartment. Patricia thought the apartment was strangely dark, given the bright streetlights outside. The soft orange glow should have shone in through the front windows. Brian and Patricia followed Susan inside and closed the door.

# chapter nineteen

Susan's condo was gorgeous. Or it would have been, if there had not been sheets of cardboard taped to the windows, blocking all the light from the floor-to-ceiling glass looking out to the street. By the windows, a row of exotic plants wilted in tasteful terra-cotta pots. Everywhere Patricia looked, the windows were covered with cardboard. There was a smell as if the trash had not been taken out in days.

She could see Susan favored a minimal, expensive style. Patricia mentally calculated the cost of Susan's furnishings. They were more expensive than Patricia's RV. That was obvious despite the strange condition of the place.

Susan tottered over to the low, tufted leather couch and collapsed on it. She kicked off her heels. She did not bother to explain the cardboard.

"Why don't I get you some water?" Brian suggested. He and Patricia shared a wordless look. They were both curious now.

"You have a lovely apartment," Patricia said to Susan while Brian went to the kitchen.

"Thank you," Susan replied. Brian returned with bottles of water. Susan did not skimp here, either. Patricia recognized the label on the water because she had once bought it by accident in New York City. A small bottle had cost her ten dollars that day.

"So, Susan, I am glad we are getting a chance to talk," said Brian. "I have been trying to reach you at your office, but your phone has gone straight to voicemail."

"My office has been closed since…since I found out about Peter," Susan said.

"You are a lawyer?" Brian asked.

"Yes. I work with investment bankers," Susan replied. She drank her water. Patricia hoped the woman was sobering up because they desperately needed answers.

"How did you know Peter?" Brian asked.

"Peter. Peter, Peter, Peter." Susan seemed to be in a storytelling mood. "We dated in college," she continued. "He could be a real playboy back then. One day he would say he wanted to marry me, the next day he would be out breaking hearts again. He tried to leave me once because he was scared of our love—how real it was. He always came crawling back to me, though sometimes he needed a little… encouragement," she said with a small smile.

"What happened?" Patricia said. She shivered to hear Susan talk about Peter this way.

"He loved me, but he wouldn't commit to me, so I broke it off," said Susan. "Besides, I needed to prove I was stronger than him. He was quite devastated," she said softly.

"Did you keep in touch after college?" asked Brian.

"No. We went our separate ways. I went to law school and Peter moved away," said Susan. "It was only in the past few years that we got back in touch."

"When you moved here to Atlanta?" asked Brian.

"Yes. I received a job offer in Atlanta that I could not pass up. The firm I work for is one of the more exclusive ones here," said Susan. She sat up straighter and seemed to take pride in herself. "I took the job. One day I was reading the paper and I saw Peter's name mentioned in an article. He was buying a restaurant and planning to open a club. I was shocked. I didn't know that Peter was in Atlanta."

"What did you do then?" asked Brian.

"I looked him up online," said Susan. "I found out where he worked and realized his office was near one of my clients. I decided to stop by and say hello."

"After so many years, and such a bad breakup, what did you think Peter's reaction would be?" asked Patricia.

"Well, I figured he would be surprised. I dropped by without calling or emailing him first," said Susan.

"How did it go?" asked Brian.

"It was better than I expected," said Susan. "We went out for lunch and it was like we had never been apart. We always did have great chemistry." She smiled as if cherishing a secret.

"Did you know Peter was married?" Patricia asked.

"Yes. Peter told me about his wife Hannah that first day," said Susan. "But he didn't talk about her a lot."

"Susan, were you having an affair with Peter?" Brian asked point-blank.

Susan opened her mouth and then closed it. She sat up and looked Brian in the eye.

"Yes," Susan said. "Jeff told you all about it, didn't he? That little backstabbing creep."

"I'm sorry, Ms. Hendron. As part of the investigation, he did tell us certain details about Peter's personal life," said Brian.

"I'm sure he had no problem spilling the beans. Jeff has never been discreet. He was a blabbermouth in college and he still is. Always getting into people's business," she said bitterly. "Always making threats like he's some kind of bargain basement mobster."

"Did Jeff say something to you about the affair? Did he threaten you?" Brian asked with concern.

"No. But I know he said something to Peter. Why else would Peter do what he did?"

"What did Peter do, Susan?" Patricia asked. Tension hovered in the room.

Susan turned to look at Patricia. Her tipsiness seemed to have left her. "He came over here crawling like a dog, his tail between his legs. I could see it in his eyes. He was going to break it off on the very night we had plans together! I knew it was Jeff's doing. Jeff hated me dating Peter in college and he hated our affair. He didn't understand that what Peter and I had was real love. Peter's marriage was just a matter of convenience. I knew it even if he refused to acknowledge that fact sometimes. That night I could see he was scared and planning to play it safe—just like he tried to do in college. Well, it was too late for safe. Besides, we already had plans. I refused to listen to a word he said until we got to the mountain."

"What mountain?" Patricia asked, startled.

"It was supposed to be a perfect night," said Susan. "We had been planning it for months. I had arranged a night of glamping for us at a park a little ways outside of Atlanta. You know, camping with all the luxuries. I had been looking forward to it for weeks. He was not going to ruin it with his stupid fears about what his stupid wife thought. When he showed up late, I knew what I had to do. I changed into sexy red lingerie under my jacket and brought a shaker full of cocktails with us in the limo. I told him this was going to be a night he would never forget." She laughed, low and full of malice.

"When we got there, I blindfolded him and led him to the campsite I had arranged to be set up. There was a gorgeous, huge linen tent with a king-sized air mattress. Chaise lounges around a fire pit. Takeout from our favorite Japanese restaurant waiting on the table with an expensive bottle of wine. It was secluded and beautiful. The kind of night where he usually couldn't keep his hands off me. He was so surprised, I knew I was winning him over, even though he refused to make love to me at first. After we ate, we sat on the chaise lounges and looked at the stars. It was very romantic." She sighed happily and leaned back into the couch.

"Was this at Stone Mountain campground, by chance?" Patricia asked.

"How did you know? Yes. It was in one of the quieter tent camping areas. I didn't want anyone to disturb us. As we sat there, I told him he could not deny his love for me any longer. He had to leave his wife so we could be together," Susan said. "I threw off my coat so he could see the red lingerie I had picked out especially for him. I got down on my knees in front of him and asked him to marry me, to take me to bed. Yes, it was backwards, he should have been the one to propose, but I did not care. I wanted to give him everything." Susan's gaze was distant. "Then I saw it in his eyes."

"What did you see?" Brian prompted her. But Susan did not reply to his question. Not yet.

"Peter told me that night was our last night together. I was furious. I got up and slapped him. Peter grabbed my wrist before I could hit him again. He looked genuinely scared—he always was a bit dramatic about these sorts of disagreements in college—and he took out his phone and said he was calling the police. I picked up the wine bottle and used it to knock the phone out of his hand. I was so furious that I swung the bottle again and it smashed into his head. He went down like a pile of bricks. We struggled, he fought me pretty hard. We were near the firepit when it happened, and I grabbed one of the big firewood logs lying there and cracked it into the side of his head. He stopped moving then. I waited for him to get up. I kept waiting. He...he never got up." Susan finally looked up at them in the near-darkness. Her eyes were wide and almost manic, but her face was calm.

She took a gulp of air. "I did not mean to kill him," Susan

gasped. "I just wanted to hurt him like he had hurt me. I needed to show him…to make him see…but then it was too late. Too late for that. When I realized he was dead, I started burning everything I could find. The limo was not around so I didn't have to care about anybody seeing. The chairs, the garbage from our dinner, the lingerie with his blood all over it. I pulled down the linen tent and wrapped up his body in it. I phoned my assistant and told her there was a change of plans, I needed my car delivered to the campground. About an hour later, she called me back from the entrance to the park. I walked to the entrance and got my car. My assistant took a taxi home. I checked to make sure there was not a trace of me or Peter left at the campsite. I put Peter…I put the body in the trunk and drove down the road. I came to a wooded area near some trails and decided to dump the body there, as if he had been hiking. I dragged it out of the car and across the road and the grass a little ways. It was heavy, so very, very heavy. I couldn't leave the tent because I was worried it would be traced back to me, so I pulled it off of the body. I was figuring out what to do next when I heard voices. I ran back to my car. I drove away and dumped everything else in the trunk in an alley dumpster in East Atlanta. I went to an all-night car wash and cleaned my car. Finally, I got back here and fell asleep, exhausted. I went to work the next day and then I stopped by Peter's office a couple of days later. I knew I had to keep up appearances…"

"That is when we saw you," said Brian.

"Yes," said Susan. "I got paranoid then. I closed up my office. I know you had cars following me, so I covered the windows. That way no one could see when I was home."

"No one was following you, Susan," said Brian quietly. "We assumed you were innocent."

"Don't lie to me," she said with venom in her voice. "I followed your taxi from the precinct to the campground, Patricia. You were getting too close to Lana and Jeff. I came back the next night to spray paint your RV, I figured I could at least get the Detective's little assistant out of the picture and slow down the investigation," Susan sneered. "You were not supposed to come home while I was there. I hit you with the end of the spray paint can. I meant to just knock you out for a moment, but I guess I hit you harder than I thought. I waited until the ambulance left and then spray painted the message."

Patricia felt her anger rise up. She felt all the pain and confusion of the last week swirling inside of her. The concussion Susan had given her was bad enough, but this confession confused her. "But why, Susan? Why would you kill Peter? He had come back to you before, why not this time?"

"Because I saw that fear in his eyes. The same fear that drove him away from me all those years ago. The fear that Jeff kept trying to shove down Peter's throat. The fear of society and his stupid wife and consequences and everything else. When I lifted that firewood above his head in that last moment, I knew. He was never going to escape the fear. He was nothing but a coward, a filthy coward of a dog, caught in a trap." Susan sat perfectly still on the couch. She did not seem to be afraid of what was coming as Brian stood up and unhooked the handcuffs from the back of his belt.

"Susan Hendron, I am placing you under arrest for the murder of Peter Sedgewick." Brian read her the familiar litany of Miranda rights as Patricia watched. *Jeff Jones spent so many years in love with this evil woman,* she thought. *What a tragic waste.*

Brian called for backup and a squad car came by and picked up Susan. Patricia felt elated that the case was solved as she and Brian walked out to his truck. They were still in their fine eveningwear.

"I hope Susan stays in jail for a long time," Patricia said.

"With what she told us, I wouldn't be surprised if she spends some time in a mental hospital first," Brian said. "She might have been lucid when she killed him, but she was very paranoid toward the end, too."

"You know, Jeff mentioned that she destroyed Peter's apartment in college when he tried to break up with her, too. It fits with the pattern of what she did here," Patricia commented. "Revenge, destruction, manipulation. This is just a very, very extreme version of it."

"You're right about that. This is why I'm glad we worked together as a team," said Brian to Patricia. He opened the car door for her. "We would not have solved it if we didn't work together." Patricia smiled, and Brian gave her a hug before she climbed into the truck.

"Would you like to join me for a celebratory dinner?" Brian asked Patricia. "I hear there's a great restaurant in north Atlanta. Very exclusive. Only the rich and famous can go there."

"I don't know…I heard about this great diner in central Atlanta," said Patricia. "I hear they have the best coffee in the city." Brian laughed, and they left Susan's house.

# chapter twenty

Patricia got up the next morning and brewed herself a pot of coffee. She took her mug to her kitchen table and sat down at her laptop. She added a few locations to her Atlanta article. It was a good article filled with fun information about Atlanta, and reading over it reminded her of the many adventures she had enjoyed. Patricia hoped the article showed off the eclecticism of Atlanta and all its little neighborhoods. After a few finishing touches, Patricia sent it off to her publisher. She laughed to herself a little bit, picturing what would happen if she added a few extra reviews to her article. Her readers did not want to hear about North County Memorial Hospital or how great the local paramedic teams were.

She sat back and put her feet up. Inside the RV felt like home. Patricia had the rest of the day to enjoy Atlanta. Her flight to Paris left the next day. She almost did not feel ready to leave. She sat there for a while and then got up. Patricia hiked to the mountain one more time and took the lift up to the top. She walked around and enjoyed the view. She even bought an ice cream cone to enjoy on her walk back down the mountain. It was a pleasant walk. The air was warm and there was a slight breeze.

Patricia finished her ice cream and walked back to her RV. She wanted nothing more than to head into Atlanta and visit a few of her favorite places again—the Botanical Gardens, the museums, maybe go shopping. However, first she needed to take care of one important task. She pulled out a scrub brush and a can of paint remover. Patricia spread the tarp under the spray paint and worked quickly to remove the ugly letters. It was hard work, and by the time she finished, she was a little sweaty and decided to hop in the shower.

As she finished blow-drying her hair afterward, her phone buzzed with a message from Brian. *Meet me for lunch?*

She smiled to herself. The night before had been fun. She and Brian ate at the diner. The waitress complimented them on their outfits. Once the adrenaline had worn off, Patricia was fatigued. Brian drove her back to the campground and told her he would be up to his neck in paperwork the next day. He had kissed her gently and left.

*I thought you had too much work to do,* she sent back to him. His reply came only moments later: *Never too busy for you.* It made her smile. They arranged a time and place to meet in Decatur.

Patricia took the bus to Decatur and arrived early. She walked around the square for a little bit and watched some teenagers try to skateboard down a railing. Patricia decided to head for the address Brian had given her and she discovered it was not just a restaurant but a live music venue. She bought her ticket for the show. She climbed up the stairs to the outside rooftop bar and sat down. Patricia ordered a beer and an appetizer. She watched a baseball game on the big screen and sipped her beer while she waited for Brian.

"Is this seat taken?" a voice asked her. Patricia turned around. Brian's familiar tall form stood beside her and he ran a hand through his wavy brown hair. She got up and hugged him. He sat down next to her.

Patricia smiled. Brian ordered a beer. Just then, Patricia's cell phone rang. It was her publisher. Patricia apologized to Brian and answered the phone. "Hello?" Patricia said.

"Hello," said Lenore. "Thanks for the article. It's perfect."

"Thank you," said Patricia.

"I'm calling about the Paris trip. I have some exciting things to tell you," Lenore said. "There is a very special opportunity for you to cover a special event taking place while you will be there. Are you interested?"

"Definitely. I'm at lunch right now, however. Can I call you back shortly?" Patricia asked.

"Okay, but we need to make a decision about this event soon," said her publisher. Patricia promised to call her back.

"Who was that?" asked Brian.

"That was Lenore, my editor and publisher," said Patricia. "She liked my article. She had something to tell me about my next assignment."

"Really? Where are you headed?" Brian asked.

"Paris," Patricia replied. Excitement filled her just saying it, even though it was bittersweet to think about leaving. "I have loved my time here in Atlanta. It's been amazing working with you on the investigation."

"Hopefully you've enjoyed more than just the work," Brian joked.

"Our stakeouts did have a habit of turning into really fun dates," said Patricia with a laugh. She gazed at Brian and his deep blue eyes looked back at her with affection.

"You'll have a great time," said Brian, breaking the silence. "But I'm hoping that maybe when you're done…you might come back to visit me."

"I'd like that very much," Patricia said. "In any case, I will have to come back to Atlanta eventually. My RV will be here waiting. I can't abandon my only home in a parking lot."

Brian grinned. "I have an idea about that. I know you keep insisting the spray paint thing wasn't my fault, but I still want to make it up to you. While you are gone, I can have your RV repainted. A friend of mine has an autobody shop. I called him today and he can refinish the paint and store it at his lot for you, too. There is security there around the clock, so your RV will be safe."

"Wow," said Patricia. "Thank you. That's so generous. But I have to get to the airport in my RV."

"I can't let my best investigative assistant just leave town. Won't you let me drive you to the airport? I can pick you up. I have the entire day off tomorrow."

Patricia agreed and felt happy thinking about the future. "Brian, I have really enjoyed my time with you."

"I have been enjoying your company, too," said Brian. "You are fun to be with."

"Not to mention I'm your lucky charm," Patricia reminded him with a laugh. They both laughed as they enjoyed their beers. They ordered lunch. It was a beautiful afternoon. Patricia had successfully finished her Atlanta assignment and fulfilled a long-held dream: to return to detective work. As a bonus, she had met a wonderful man who seemed to like her back, too.

They finished their meal and stood to go to the live music stage. Brian took her hand as they walked down the stairs and found seats side by side at a small table.

"Can I tell you something?" Brian said, leaning in close. She looked up at him. "You're not just my lucky charm. You're a really great detective. I couldn't have solved this case without your help."

"Thank you," said Patricia. She smiled and put her head on Brian's shoulder. The singer came out and everyone clapped. He was from Boston, and Patricia recognized him from his career with a power pop group back in the nineties. His solo work was more biographical and jangly now. It reminded Patricia of the psychedelic sixties bands and some of the early eighties bands she loved. When a particularly sweet song came on, Brian took her hand and they stood to sway and dance together for a little while.

After the concert, Patricia walked contentedly with Brian. He drove her back to her RV. They hugged for a few minutes and then Brian kissed her goodnight. It was a slow, sweet kiss. When he pulled away, Patricia had tears in her eyes. Brian wiped them away and kissed her again.

"Well, I guess I need to pack for my next adventure," Patricia said.

"Yes," said Brian. "And I'll be here to pick you up tomorrow." Patricia held on to Brian for a while. Then she let go. Patricia said goodnight and Brian drove away.

Happy and tired, she went into her RV and turned on her laptop. She looked up the weather for springtime in Paris and started to pack as much as she could into two suitcases. She was not sure how long she would be in Paris, so she tended to over-pack. When she was done packing, Patricia had a sudden thought. *I never called Lenore back about that event.* She grabbed her phone and sent Lenore a text message, hoping it was not too late. She told her she was definitely interested, whatever it was. There was no answer immediately, so she resolved to call Lenore from the airport.

Finally, Patricia crawled into her bed. She was tired from walking all day and she quickly fell asleep and dreamed about the Eiffel Tower.

# chapter twenty-one

The next morning, Patricia woke up bright and early. She made some breakfast and washed her dishes. She checked around the RV and made sure there were no open containers of food. She grabbed the food that was left in her refrigerator and put it in a bag. She looked through her cabinets and grabbed some of that food, too. She carried the bags over to Tom and Valerie's RV. It had been dark when she got back the night before, so she had not gone over. Patricia knocked gently on the door. It flew open, and Valerie bounded out.

"Congratulations on solving the case," she said and hugged Patricia. Patricia smiled.

"Thank you, Valerie," she said.

"It is all over the news today," said Valerie. "Brian's name was mentioned on television a couple of times."

"That will be great for his career," said Patricia.

"What's in the bags?" Valerie asked.

"It's the food from my refrigerator and some from my pantry," said Patricia. "I am going to Paris and I do not want it to go to waste. Can you use it?"

"You are going to Paris?" Valerie asked in awe. "When do you leave?"

"I will be flying out later this afternoon," Patricia said.

"I'm so excited for you. What about Brian?" Valerie asked.

"He is happy for me, too," said Patricia. Valerie hugged her again. Tom came out of the RV and asked what was going on. Valerie told him and took the bags from Patricia. Tom gave Patricia a hug and congratulated her.

"Thank you. I could not have survived this crazy trip without the two of you. You have been so sweet. I have had a wonderful time being your neighbor," said Patricia.

"You sure did give us a few scares," said Tom, shaking his head. "I'm just glad that everything worked out. After all my worries, it turned out the detective was right about everything and I should not have worried about you. Seems like he's a pretty decent guy, too."

Patricia smiled. "I will miss you two so much."

"Well, who knows where you will end up after Paris," said Valerie. "Our paths may cross again in the future."

"I would like that," said Patricia. She made sure she had both Tom and Valerie's numbers. Valerie told her to send them pictures from Paris.

"What is going to happen to your RV?" asked Tom.

"Brian's friend will take it to his shop and fix it," said Patricia. "He said it will be good as new when I'm done traveling in Paris. It will be waiting for me when I get back."

"The RV will not be the only thing waiting for you," Tom winked. Patricia blushed.

"How are you getting to the airport?" Valerie asked. "Do you need a ride?"

"No, Brian is going to pick me up," said Patricia.

"That is nice of him," said Valerie.

"Yes, it is," said Patricia. "He made me promise to come back to see him. He even told me I was a good detective."

"I knew you were all along," said Valerie. Patricia laughed. They hugged goodbye and Patricia walked back to her RV. She opened her laptop and perused the news. The conclusion of the investigation was bringing Brian the credit he deserved. There was even mention of a promotion in one of the articles. Patricia was proud of Brian. She was glad she had been a small part of the investigation. A few minutes later, Patricia heard Brian's truck. She got up and went outside. There was another person in the truck with Brian. It was a good-looking young man.

"Patricia, this is Wesley. He is the one who will be taking care of your RV for you," said Brian. Wesley held out his hand and Patricia shook it.

"He is really experienced with vehicle restoration. I promise he will drive it just as safely as you would," said Brian.

"Thank you so much, Wesley," said Patricia. "Let me make sure I have everything I need for my trip." Patricia went back inside and gathered up her things. She took her suitcases and her small bag outside. Patricia grabbed her keys. She took the spare keys off her key ring and handed them to Wesley.

"Now you take good care of my baby," Patricia said. "We have been through a lot together." Brian smiled.

"I will take good care of her, ma'am," said Wesley.

"If he doesn't, I will arrest him," Brian joked. They all laughed.

"How long will you be gone?" Wesley asked.

"I am not sure," said Patricia. "There is a special event my editor wants me to cover. She has not told me yet what it is."

"Well, don't worry about how long it takes," said Wesley. "Your RV can stay with me for as long as necessary."

"Thank you very much," said Patricia.

"You're welcome," said Wesley. He climbed into the driver's seat and waved from the window as he pulled out into the road and drove away.

"Are you sure you have everything?" asked Brian. Patricia looked around. Her campsite was completely empty now.

"Yes. It's a little early to head right to the airport," Patricia said.

"I thought we would stop for lunch on the way. There is a place you have not gotten to yet," said Brian. "It's one of my favorites."

"Where is it?" asked Patricia.

"It is by the old baseball field," said Brian. Brian picked up Patricia's suitcases and loaded them in the truck. He opened Patricia's door for her and helped her in. They waved to Tom and Valerie as they drove past, and Brian steered the truck towards southern Atlanta.

About twenty minutes later, Brian pulled into the restaurant. It was the Varsity, an old-fashioned diner with drive-in order stalls and outdoor tables.

"They are famous for their hotdogs and milkshakes," said Brian. Patricia smiled. It was like stepping back into the fifties.

"This is my kind of restaurant," Patricia said. They went inside. Brian and Patricia ordered at the front counter. Patricia scanned the menu and ordered a hotdog with chili and a chocolate milkshake. They got their food and Brian found them a table by the windows. Patricia tried her hotdog.

"This is fantastic," she said to Brian.

"I knew you would like it," he said. Patricia savored her milkshake as well. It was a warm day.

"Your name was mentioned on television today," said Patricia.

"Wesley told me that too," said Brian.

"Have you watched the news reports?" Patricia asked.

"No, I have not," said Brian. "I know what happened. We lived it. I do not need to hear what people are saying about me."

"Well, I like what they are saying, and I am very proud of you," said Patricia.

"I could not have done it without you," said Brian. Patricia smiled.

They finished their meal and Patricia looked out the window at the Atlanta skyline. The gold dome of the capital building shone in the bright sun. Patricia had been all over the city, but she knew there were other places she had to visit. Perhaps that was just another excuse to come back, Patricia realized happily. Brian took their empty wrappers and threw them away.

"Is it time to go to the airport?" Patricia asked. She felt reluctant.

"Yes, it is," said Brian. Patricia sighed. He held her hand as they walked to Brian's truck. Before Patricia got in, Brian pulled her close. He held her and kissed her tenderly.

"You are taking part of my heart with you to Paris," Brian said. "Keep it safe." Patricia could not help but start crying. Brian smiled and held her close.

"You will have a great time in Paris," he said. "Heck, you'll probably meet some tall, handsome foreigner and forget all about me."

"Not a chance, Detective," Patricia answered. She held him close and he wiped her tears away. She kissed him again and then got into the truck.

"I did not want to do that at the airport," said Brian.

"I appreciate that," said Patricia. Her heart ached a little bit. She was also starting to get anxious about her flight. Patricia loved to fly, but the airport was always a hassle. Brian parked at the airport and carried her bags for her to the check-in kiosk and waited while she printed her boarding pass. When she had checked her bags in, she thanked Brian.

"You have made my life fun and exciting," she told Brian. "Thank you."

"You are the perfect partner," said Brian. "Thank you." They kissed goodbye. Patricia wanted to linger in the kiss, but Brian had to get back to the office and she had a plane to catch. Brian turned to go, and Patricia wiped the tears from her eyes. She waved, then turned around and went through security.

After fifteen minutes, she was on the other side. She checked her tickets and boarded the underground transport to her gate. She got off the train and found her waiting area. Patricia had some time so she wandered around the stores in the airport. There was plenty to see and Patricia felt herself calming down. She was looking forward to seeing Paris. It was going to be a long flight, but Patricia was prepared. She had her novel and her laptop.

Patricia's eye was caught by a newspaper. It was the local Atlanta paper. The story about the conclusion to the investigation of Peter's murder featured as the top headline. Patricia purchased the paper and put it in her bag. *For my future scrapbook,* Patricia thought. She smiled and walked back to the gate. The attendants were getting ready to start boarding. Patricia got in line and looked out the window. Her plane on the tarmac looked good. It was a larger plane, which made Patricia happy. When she got to the front of the line the attendant scanned her ticket and welcomed her aboard the plane. Patricia wheeled her carryon down the hallway to the plane.

Another attendant pointed out her seat in first class. Patricia made a mental note to thank Lenore for this special luxury. The attendant offered Patricia a drink and a snack. Patricia also asked for and received a pillow and blanket. Patricia looked out the window. She was going to miss Brian and Atlanta, but she was looking forward to her new adventure.

She took out her phone to turn it off. Patricia found a message from Lenore about the special event assignment and grinned as she read the details. She did not have time to think about it because everyone was instructed to buckle in for the safety demonstration. Soon the plane started down the runway and took off. Patricia's stomach flew up and then unknotted. They were in the air.

"Have you been to Paris before?" the older woman in the next seat asked Patricia.

"No," said Patricia. "This is my first time."

"Mine too," said the older woman. "What a wonderful adventure."

"Yes, indeed," Patricia agreed. She thought ahead to Paris with excitement and anticipation bubbling inside. Outside her window, Atlanta spread out like a beautiful jewel in the sun. She smiled knowing that Brian was somewhere down there, working hard. *You are taking part of my heart with you to Paris,* he had said. It gave her a sweet, warm feeling in her heart. She relaxed and settled in for the flight. It was going to be an exciting trip.

# more from wendy

Alaska Cozy Mystery Series

Maple Hills Cozy Series

Sweeeetfern Harbor Cozy Series

Sweet Peach Cozy Series

Sweet Shop Cozy Series

Twin Berry Bakery Series

# about wendy meadows

Wendy Meadows is a USA Today bestselling author whose stories showcase women sleuths. To date, she has published dozens of books, which include her popular Sweetfern Harbor series, Sweet Peach Bakery series, and Alaska Cozy series, to name a few. She lives in the "Granite State" with her husband, two sons, two mini pigs and a lovable Labradoodle.

Join Wendy's newsletter to stay up-to-date with new releases. As a subscriber, you'll also get BLACKVINE MANOR, the complete series, for FREE!

**Join Wendy's Newsletter Here**

wendymeadows.com/cozy

www.ingramcontent.com/pod-product-compliance
Ingram Content Group UK Ltd.
Pitfield, Milton Keynes, MK11 3LW, UK
UKHW021936190726
13853UKWH00004B/1486